CONTENTS

INTRODUCTION TO THIS MYSTERY!

Trapped in a magical Renaissance Faire and accused of murder. Huzzah!

When Adelaide "Laidey" Ryan dragged herself off the couch for a date at the Renaissance Faire, she didn't expect to run into her cheating ex-fiancé. The day only gets better when she winds up trapped on the magical grounds and discovers she's a witch. And the best part? She's charged with a homicide she didn't commit.

With the "help" of a snarky talking cat, this former Pilates teacher will have to wade through a turkey-leg sized list of suspects to find the real killer, all while juggling her new job as a broom maker's apprentice. Despite her troubles, there's a dashingly handsome pirate captain who has her heart aflutter. But time is running out on her sleuthing, and the lazy sheriff is eager to march her to the gallows.

Can Laidey catch the murderer, or will her snooping make her Faire game for the killer?

Much A'Broom About Nothing is the first book in the humorous paranormal cozy series, Magical Renaissance Faire Mysteries. If you like snarky heroines, twisty mysteries, and a hint of romance, you'll love curling up with Erin Johnson's charming whodunit.

Enjoy *Much A'Broom About Nothing* and solve a sweeping mystery today!

THE BIRDS!

The big brown chicken pecked at the top left square and beat my date—for the fifth time in a row—at tic-tac-toe.

"How? How does she do it? She's a genius!" Cliff shook his head, a huge grin on his face as he slow clapped for the star of the Hen Pecked booth.

Her keeper, a man in pantaloons and a feathered cap, swept forward. "Care to challenge the feathered phenomenon in another battle of the wits?"

I scrunched up my nose. "Er... maybe we should be moving on? Lots more Ren Faire to see."

I'd been standing around in the bright summer sun while Cliff stared down poultry for the last fifteen minutes, and I was ready to move on. Sweat ran down my back, and my stinging shoulders clued me in that I was skipping right over tanned and straight to burned. Also, I'd begun to suspect that my date had an unhealthy obsession with birds.

I'd thought "animal lover" on his online profile sounded endearing, and when he'd talked about birding on our first date, I'd thought "what a unique hobby." Sure, the somewhat dorky Cliff wasn't exactly my "ideal" man, but my mom had convinced me to give him another chance, hence our second date at the Renaissance Faire.

His choice.

Maybe the nice, eager Cliff was what I needed after who I'd *thought* was my ideal man broke my heart and pushed me into a downward spiral of depression and existential despair.

Cliff winced as he debated playing another game with a bird or spending time with me, his human date. He looked from me to the chicken.

Please don't pick the chicken.

"Ooh, it's tempting, but…" He consulted the time on his phone as he rose from the wooden stool in front of the chicken's enclosure. "Yikes! It's nearly one o'clock—almost time for the falconer show." He waggled his brows at me. "Better get a move on— trust me, you *don't* want to miss this."

Unhealthy bird obsession confirmed.

"You mean, it's nearly one o'*cluck*?" Pantaloons held up a finger and waggled his brows.

"Ha!" Cliff slapped his thigh while I managed a weak grin.

"Heh." If I had to listen to Pantaloons deliver one more bird pun…

"Eh, so yer *chickening* out, young squire?" He planted his hands on his hips.

Cliff chuckled, like he couldn't believe this man's wit. "You know, sir, you're a real hoot." He raised his brows over his glasses. "Get it? Hoot? Like an owl?"

Pantaloons doubled over, laughing.

Kill me.

Cliff grabbed my hand and dragged me along before I could escape. We threaded through the packed throng of Fairegoers, many of them decked out in fairy wings, chain link armor, and corsets. I'd never been to the Faire and was equal parts intrigued and confused by the mishmash of pirates, elves, peasants, and fairies. I'd even seen a clan of ninjas wandering through. Since I'd *seen* them, they clearly needed to work on their stealth training.

While I would've liked to browse the little shops that hocked leather masks, fortunes, and ceramic mugs, Cliff had other plans for us.

"Did you know that falcons can spot their prey from a mile away?" Cliff glanced over his shoulder at me as we fought the current.

"Nice." That was a handy skill. I wish I could've spotted a cheater from a mile away. Would've come in handy with my ex-fiancé.

"And just wait till the falconer tosses the treat in

3

the air—the falcons catch it!" He winced. "Hope I didn't spoil it for you."

If I said it had, would it get me out of having to watch the show? I sucked in a breath and mentally scolded myself. *Adelaide Ryan, you are to stay positive. You are on a date, wearing pants that aren't crumb-covered sweats, and you brushed your teeth today.* As I used to remind my Pilates clients, *progress—not perfection.*

Cliff and I ducked down a side lane where a woman in a long dress waved us on. "Show's starting! Come see the amazing falconer, Brandon Bonmarito, and his soaring show, Fight and Flight!"

Was everything here a pun?

We slid into the back of the throng just in time to catch the opening.

"Gather round! And I shall tell ye of these magnificent birds of prey!" The falconer's voluminous sleeve ended in a leather glove, where a lovely black speckled falcon perched.

The crowd applauded, but I frowned up at my date. Had he just mouthed the falconer's speech word for word?

Unease washed over me. "How many times have you seen this show?"

Cliff didn't bother looking at me, his shining eyes glued to the stage. "This season?"

That meant "too many" times. A wave of anxiety tightened my stomach as I recalled a tidbit from his profile that mentioned he was a "Falconer Groupie." I'd assumed Falconer was an indie band I'd never heard of. Now, I knew.

Cliff's hand clasped around mine. "Let's get closer."

I shot other Fairegoers apologetic smiles as Cliff tugged me past them toward the stage.

"Falconry has oft been referred to as the—"

"King's sport!" Cliff shouted in tandem with the man on stage.

The falconer, who I had to admit was pretty easy on the eyes, scanned the crowd. His shoulders slumped when he spotted my date. "Greetings, Cliff."

My date waved his entire arm overhead as those around us turned to stare. My cheeks burned hot with embarrassment as I tried to yank my hand free from his. This was clearly not going to work out. It was time to pull the ripcord.

"Laidey?"

I felt as though a bucket of ice water had just been dumped over my head. I knew that voice. Almost against my will, I looked to my left.

My ex-fiancé, handsome as ever, stood with his arm wrapped around the waist of the woman he'd left me for. I wanted to die.

I plastered on a pained smile and tried to pry my hand from Cliff's grip. "Chad... hey!" I managed to wrench my hand free and lurched sideways.

"You okay, Laidey?" Cliff finally looked away

from his precious birds to eye me with concern at exactly the wrong time.

"Oh." Chad gestured between Cliff and me with his free hand. "Is this— Are you on a date?"

I shook my head no as Cliff nodded yes.

Meredith—I hated that I knew her name—smirked. The gall. She and Chad looked like they were made for each other—both lean, tanned, and tall—which only made me feel worse.

They'd met in their weekend cycling group. Saturday rides had turned into weekend trips and races away. I clenched my jaw so hard I feared I might break a tooth. Turned out bikes weren't the only thing ol' Meredith was riding—hey o!

While I'd never shared Chad's passion for cycling, I used to be fit and lean, too. I was a Pilates teacher, and I'd had the body to prove it, even after I'd opened my own studio and had to fight to find time to work out. I'd have thought it would be easy, but everything changed after I opened my own place. I loved teaching because I loved helping people get fit, healthy, and confident.

But owning my own studio meant almost no time on the mat, and overtime behind the desk. It became a nightmare of managing staff, marketing, and running numbers. But I stuck with it, because Adelaide Ryan was no quitter! That was, until about eight months ago, when I'd caught Chad cheating on me.

Instead of begging my forgiveness, he'd called off our engagement and flooded Instagram with pics of him and Meredith in new-love bliss. I'd taken a different tack, struggling to crawl from my bed to the couch each day, and had become such a shut-in that my already fair skin now practically glowed in the dark. I went from healthy smoothies and daily workouts to bingeing bags of potato chips and lifting the TV remote to pick a Netflix series for exercise.

So when one of my teachers offered to buy the studio from me, I jumped at the opportunity for a new start. I'd lost my love of managing the studio long ago, but Chad's betrayal and my subsequent lack of motivation to do anything really capped it off. It'd been three months since I handed over the keys, but I still had yet to figure out what I was going to do with my life.

So in answer to my ex's question, yes, I was doing *so good*.

Heat flushed up my neck and chest as I stood, mortified, next to my bird-obsessed date and faced off my ex-fiancé and his unfairly beautiful new girl-friend. She stood there with a flower crown atop her perfect beach waves, eyeing me with undisguised pity.

She shot me a simpering smile as Chad frowned, concerned. "How you holding up?"

I raised my brows. *Seriously?* How did he *think* I was holding up? I balled my hands into trembling fists as I willed myself to keep it together. One of the core tenets of Pilates was control—and my last bit of it snapped.

Energy flooded through me, cool and heady and unlike anything I'd ever experienced before. Every cell of my body tingled, and time slowed. Was I losing control? Or was I strangely more in command than I'd ever been?

As if in slow motion, one of the falcons soared overhead—*right* over the heads of Chad and Meredith. Somehow, I knew what was about to happen. Because somehow, I was *making* it happen.

Do it, I willed the bird mentally.

I swear it winked at me.

I curled my lip into a wry smile as a white, runny dropping plummeted from the sky and splattered on my ex's and Meredith's heads.

"*E*w!" Chad's side piece shrieked, and my ex grimaced. Time returned to normal speed.

The crowd chuckled, and the falconer called from the stage, "The birds are trained but not housebroken!"

The crowd laughed harder.

I probably should've been reveling in Chad and Meredith's embarrassment. Instead, I gasped for breath, on the verge of hyperventilating. Had I just exacted revenge on my ex by somehow willing a falcon to defecate on his stupid head? That was crazy, right? Was I crazy?

My chest heaved as I turned to Cliff. This whole get-out-of-the-house adventure had been great, but clearly I'd pushed myself too hard to move on and was losing it. Time to retreat to the safety of my couch and elastic waistbands. "Cliff…"

He blinked at me from behind his glasses as I sought the right words to express that this wasn't going to work out. Unfortunately, I was too freaked out by the bird/frozen time incident to be polite.

"Bye forever."

I cast one last furtive glance at my ex and his new girl as they whimpered and attempted to blot bird droppings out of their hair. Even if I was losing my mind, seeing their mortified faces might've been worth it. As I stumbled away from the falconer, no one paid me any attention.

Everyone's eyes stayed fixed on the stage and the birds—all except for a lone pirate who lounged near the entrance. He leaned against a post, arms crossed, and watched me leave with dark eyes. His impressively thick mustache twitched upward with a knowing smirk. His gaze was both flattering and unnerving.

I hurried past him and disappeared into the crowd in the lane. I planned to go home and lick my wounds. But on my way to the exit, I found myself rushing up to the mead booth and double fisting a couple of tankards in an attempt to drown out all memories of that awkward encounter and my possible power over birds.

"Shouldn't drink on an empty stomach," I reprimanded myself, which led to a feast of giant turkey legs, which in turn led to more grog, and then more feasting. The afternoon passed in a blur. I was pretty sure I attended a jousting match, where I screamed "girl power" at a dark-haired female knight with a dove on her shoulder, and might've even gotten a henna tramp stamp on my lower back.

I was stumbling my way over to the candy house that looked straight out of Hansel and Gretel when the handsome pirate from the falcon show suddenly stepped in front of me.

I lurched back and blinked up at him. As he came into focus—sort of—I admired him. His thick black locks were tied back in a low ponytail, leather straps crossed his broad chest, and again, that mustache! He could give Tom Selleck a run for his money.

I hiccuped and swayed on my feet. "Hey, sailor."

He raised a thick brow and grinned. "It's Captain, actually."

His voice was deep and slightly gravelly. I pretended to tip my nonexistent hat. "Apologies, good sir."

He fought a smile, then cleared his throat and glanced over his shoulder. "I couldn't help but notice you charting a course straight for the Crooked Confectioner."

I leaned past him to look at the enticing house that appeared to be made of gumdrops, frosting, and gingerbread. A short, grandmotherly old woman who looked like the incarnation of Mother Goose herself stood in front of the door and smiled warmly at me.

Come eat some candy, Adelaide?

She and her candy house were literally calling my name.

"Thanks for reminding me." I staggered past, but the handsome pirate leaped directly into my path, cutting me off again.

I frowned up at him and hiccuped. "Hey."

He shot a furtive glance back at the gingerbread house, then bent closer and lowered his voice. "A word to the wise—stay clear of the Crooked Confectioner. Rocky shores ahead, if you catch my drift?"

"Not at all."

Come, child.

I swayed on my drunken feet. "I want candy."

The pirate nodded, which sent the feather on his impressive triangle-shaped hat bobbing. "Of course, Pomelo's confections call to all magical folk, but you mustn't eat any—they're cursed."

I hiccuped again and giggled. "Kudos on this whole backstory." I twirled a finger. "Very creative." I leaned closer and grinned. "Do you run a rival candy shop or something?"

"Listen, I saw what you did." He raised his brows and leveled me with a significant look.

Heat rushed up my throat, and I blinked furiously. "Look, they were already done with them, okay? They were just going to get thrown away!"

He frowned and shot me a quizzical look. Maybe

he *hadn't* seen me devour that half-eaten basket of fries a family left behind.

"I was referring to the incident with the falcon." He smirked. "Nice aim, by the way. Quite impressive."

My heart stopped. "That's not funny." I'd played along with his "magical" warnings about cursed candy up till now. It was all part of the act, right? Everyone at the Faire stayed in character. But this was going too far. "You didn't see anything, okay? I don't know what you're talking about."

I shoved past him and didn't look back. My heart raced and my head spun with more than just a few tankards of grog. This wasn't happening. There was no such thing as magic or cursed candy, and I was going to prove it.

I handed the last of my cash over to the kindly old woman, and she passed me a waxed paper bag full of sugary confections. I ducked back into the crowd as I popped a gummy worm in my mouth. The sour sugary goodness was about the tastiest thing I'd ever eaten. I looked back to wave my thanks at the little old lady but was startled to find she'd left and been replaced by what must've been her scarier, much older sister. Instead of a kindly smile, the crooked crone leered and cackled.

Yikes!

I hurried away and spent the next couple of hours browsing the shops as I sobered up, but eventually the sun dipped below the horizon and the crowd thinned.

CLANG CLANG CLANG!

"Faire's closing!"

The mead booth shuttered their windows, and the petite fairies hawking silk wings packed up their wares. I filed with the rest of the herd toward the exit and the parking lot beyond. About a dozen men and women stood just inside the gates, serenading the leaving Fairegoers while a man in tights accompanied them on the lute.

"Fare thee well, as ye leave the Faire,

Thanks for coming, now make yourself scarce!"

A large man in a bright fuchsia vest and neon orange tights stood on the wall above the big gates, shouting over the singing at the exiting patrons.

"Thanks for the money, come spend some more soon! Take me with you!"

I winced as I neared the gates, his booming voice deafening. Would it be rude to plug my ears? I waited my turn as I shuffled forward, then finally reached the gates and—

"Ow!"

I stumbled back and rubbed my nose, looking around for whatever I'd just slammed face-first into. I blinked as my eyes teared up. Maybe I hadn't been paying attention and had just run into the guy in front of me?

The crowd swarmed around me out the gates

and into the parking lot, where headlights flashed on in the deepening dusk. I shook it off and started forward but was again thrown back. This time I stumbled and fell hard on my bottom. I got a few looks from the last leaving stragglers.

Wincing, I dragged myself to my feet and dusted off my jeans. What the heck was going on? It was almost like I'd run into an invisible force field—but everyone *else* was passing through just fine. I picked myself up and, more carefully this time, inched forward, arms outstretched. The hairs on my arms rose, lifted by static electricity, and my fingertips tingled. What was this? I licked my lips and shuffled forward as cars peeled out of the parking lot beyond the gate.

My fingertips pressed against something hard and icy hot. I pushed with my palms, which tingled with little zaps of electricity. When the invisible barrier didn't give, I shoved harder, then leaned my shoulder into it and rammed with my whole body weight. The unseen forcefield crackled and threw me back, rippling and somewhat iridescent for a moment before once again becoming clear as glass.

I gaped. What in the world was going on?

The loud man in the even louder clothes peered down at me from the top of the gates, then straightened and shouted, "We've got another one!"

A couple of guys in vests walked the huge,

15

wooden gates closed. My heart thundered in my chest as I rushed toward the exit.

"Wait! Wait—I need to leave!"

The closest guy snorted. "Yeah, you and all the rest of us stuck in this cursed kingdom." They closed the gates and laid a heavy wooden beam across them. Panic seized me as I whirled around.

The choir beside the gate continued to sing along with the lute player's strumming.

"Welcome to the Elbion Faire, best not to make a fuss!"

My head swam. Were they singing at me?

The men and women swayed in time. "'Cause you're stuck till the end of days, just like the rest of us! Huzzah!"

The music ended, and the choir broke up. The man atop the gate threw his head back and boomed, "I say again! The population of Elbion has just increased by one!"

What. Is. Happening.

A woman with curly, bright orange hair stalked toward me. She swiped a hand toward the man on the gate. "Ah, keep yer 'at on, Charlie. I'll claim 'er, bruv."

The middle-aged woman slung an arm around my shoulders like we were old friends and steered me away from the gates. I threw a panicked glance back at the exit and tried to dig my heels in, but the woman was too strong. She pulled me along with her.

"Om Macy Mulligan. Was yer name, luv?" She pointed at me with a fingerless glove-clad hand.

I gulped. This had to be some kind of mead-induced hallucination, right? "A-Adelaide." I struggled to swallow, my mouth dry. "Everyone calls me Laidey."

"Oh, I've go' meself a lady, ay? La-di-dah!" Macy threw her head back and cackled, revealing a few missing teeth. "Wel'ome to Elbion, deary—yer one of us now."

MACY MULLIGAN

$\mathcal{M}$acy Mulligan steered me through the darkening lanes of the Renaissance Faire, her surprisingly strong arm clamped around my shoulders. Some burly men with swords on their hips filed into a bright, boisterous tavern with a wooden sign above the door that read Wilde's Abbey.

One of the men raised a bushy brow as we passed. "Yeh coming, Macy?"

"Soon 'nuff, luv. Jus' got to get this one squared 'way." She shook me like a rag doll.

"Where are we going?" My chest heaved. "What's happening to me? Why couldn't I leave?"

She cackled. "Ate the ol' lady's candy, did ya?"

I cast back through my racing, possibly hungover mind. "The candy from the gingerbread house? I might've eaten some, yes." By "some" I meant a small backpack's worth.

"Then yer trapped, deary, just like the rest of us. There's a curse on the Faire."

I gawked. "That nice old lady cursed me?"

"The ol' hag, Pomelo Turrón, runs the Crooked Confectioner. If yer magical and eat her candy —*bang*!"

I startled.

"Ya can never leave. The hag brings in new blood, but the curse on the Faire itself?" Macy shook her head, which sent her flaming orange curls bouncing. "Nah, tha's someone else's doin'."

"There's been a mistake, then. I'm not magical." I couldn't believe I was arguing these terms as though they were real.

Macy tugged at the ribbon lacing the front of her corset. "Yes, yeh are, deary. Didn't ya know?"

I just stared as a response, and she threw her head back and cackled.

"Well, tha's a laugh! Ain't yer family magical then?"

"My grandma had 'visions,' but she was pretty out there." I frowned. What if MeeMaw *hadn't* been off her rocker? I shook myself. No. No way was any of this magic stuff real.

Macy guided me toward an open field dotted with old-fashioned caravans, tree houses linked by rope bridges, and peaked tents. Suddenly, I realized what was happening!

I threw my head back and wailed, "Help! HELP! I've been kidnapped!"

Macy clamped a hand over my mouth and pulled me close. She narrowed her eyes. "None of tha', luv. It ain't true, and it won't do you no good no hows."

She released me and I scraped my tongue over the roof of my mouth. *Gross.* Her fingerless gloves tasted like old beer and dirt. Plus, her reaction had only confirmed my worst fears. I'd definitely been kidnapped.

We passed some Vikings making s'mores around a campfire and a group of tall, elegant elves playing lyres. No one had spared me more than a quick glance when I screamed for help. Was the whole Faire in on it?

Then again, kidnapping didn't explain the invisible forcefield at the gate.

Macy turned me left, down a narrow dirt lane with twinkle lights strung overhead between the trees, and then we cut across the soft grassy field between striped tents.

"Now that yer 'ere, you'll be needin' a place to sleep, plus food and drink..." Macy raised a thin brow. "How many doubloons do you got?"

I shook my head. Aside from some pocket change, I'd spent everything I'd pulled from the ATM on turkey legs and mead.

"Wha? None? And ya ain't got a clan to take ya' in neither. *Tsk, tsk.*" Macy shook her head. "Why, ya wouldn't last the night by yerself."

"I wouldn't?"

"I'll tell ya what then, I'll do ya a big favor." We came to an abrupt stop outside a peaked green-and-yellow-striped tent. A few others nearby glowed from the inside, silhouetting their pointy-eared occupants.

Macy spun me to face her and clamped a vise-like hand on my shoulder.

I winced.

"Lucky you that I've got such a big heart!" She swept a lean, muscled arm toward the tent, and the flaps flew open.

I gawked—how'd she do that?

A cat mewed from inside.

"Hold yer 'orses!" she barked before softening her voice and turning back to me. Her eyes weren't soft though. They were hard—like a lion fixed on its prey.

"Yeh can sleep in me tent, and I'll give ya food, shelter, and protection. I'll even let ya work off yer debt."

She shoved me into the yurt-sized tent and marched me over to two cages on the dirt ground. A chubby black cat with green eyes lay on its back in the bigger, wooden cage while two white mice scampered about in the smaller glass one beside it.

Both enclosures looked much too small for the animals, and neither had any food or water. Had Macy left them alone like this all day? As an animal lover, I'd longed to have a cat or dog, but with my long hours at work, I knew it wouldn't be fair to them. And then, after I sold the Pilates studio, I'd barely been able to keep *myself* alive, much less another living creature.

Still… I was pretty sure I'd have done a better job than Macy.

"Are these your pets?"

She scoffed. "They're my act."

I raised a brow, and her eyes grew round.

"Ya mean to tell me you ain't never 'eard of the World Famous Cat and Mouse Show?"

Somehow I doubted the "world famous" part.

Macy strutted forward and kicked the cat's cage with the toe of her boot.

"Pardon thee!"

The world swayed, and I pointed. "Did the—did the cat just talk?"

He flopped to his side and gave me a lazy blink. "'Tis rude to speaketh of me as if I am not here."

I gaped.

Macy planted a booted foot on top of the cat's cage, Captain Morgan-style, and the cat shot her a withering glance. "I make 'em do tricks and folks laugh, an' the harder they laugh, the more they tip— remember that."

I frowned. "Why?"

"'Cause it's part of yer job now." Macy stomped over to a wooden trunk, fished out a pot and powder puff, then rouged her cheeks to form perfectly round, pink circles.

It was a look.

She held up a hand mirror and admired her reflection. "You'll feed 'em, teach 'em new tricks, clean up after 'em, round up an audience for me performances—that's twice a day. I got the best times, since I'm the Faire's most popular act. *And* you'll 'ave to swat the birds away, of course."

"Birds?"

Macy adjusted "the girls" so that they spilled even further out of her corset. Someone had a hot date.

"The falconer's birds are always swoopin' by, tryin' to eat my act!" She shook a finger. "That man needs to keep a better 'old over them or I'll be makin' crow and falcon pie one of these days."

"You'll have to give me the recipe."

She ignored me and headed for the exit.

"Do not neglect to feed us again, or we shan't have the necessary 'pep' for the morrow's show," the cat drawled in his deep voice.

Macy waved a hand, and water and food dishes appeared in the cages.

I gasped. "Are you a witch?"

The mice eagerly snatched up pieces of corn and

furiously nibbled, but the cat merely sniffed his bowl. "This chicken smelleth past its time."

Macy planted her hands on her ample hips. "Well, it's all you're gettin', so you'll eat it and you'll like it."

She sounded like an eviler version of my mom, growing up.

"See ya." Macy stomped toward the tent flaps, and I lurched after her. Call me Stockholm Syndrome-ed, but she was my only lifeline in this crazy situation.

"Wait—where are you going?"

Macy snorted. "To the pub, where else?"

My heart raced. It appeared cats could talk and witches were real, and if that was the case, then what other dangerous creatures were wandering about outside the tent's thin silk walls?

"What about me?"

Macy shrugged. "What about you?"

"What am I supposed to do? Am I in danger? What if someone comes to the—"

Macy gripped my shoulders and steered me backwards. I stumbled and glanced over my shoulder. She stopped me directly in front of the lumpy pile of blankets on the ground.

"Get some sleep." She raised her pencil-thin brows. "You've got a big day tomorrow."

I scoffed. "Sleep?" No way was I even going to close my eyes.

Macy grumbled to herself and trudged back over

to the chest. She pulled out a small purple pouch and returned with it resting in her palm.

"What's that?"

She tugged the drawstring open, grabbed a pinch of the sparkly grains inside, then arched a brow. "Fairy dust. Expensive stuff, hard to get—I'll add it to your debt."

"What's it for?"

"You'll sleep like a changeling."

She threw the dust in my face, and I scrunched my eyes shut—*ow*! Macy shoved me hard in the chest, and I fell backwards onto the pallet bed. The second my head hit the straw mattress, the world went black.

"WAKE UP, HUMAN!"

A tiny furry paw batted my cheek.

I blinked, the world blurry and bright.

"Finally," the low voice drawled.

Chad? I was back in my own bed with my fiancé, and everything was right as rain. I stretched, feeling perfectly rested. That fairy dust had really done the trick.

Wait... fairy powder? I shot upright, and the black cat on my chest sprang away with an indignant yowl.

"Oh no, oh no, oh no." I scrubbed at my eyes,

hoping that when I opened them again, the cat and the yurt would just be a bad nightmare.

"You should probably summon the sheriff."

Chest heaving, I dropped my hands and peeled an eye open. Bright morning sunshine shone through the tent as the cat rubbed his cheek against the corner of the empty mouse cage. Where were the mice?

"Did you eat them?"

"Hardly. They were gone when I awoke."

Likely story. I gulped and tried to make sense of what the cat had said a moment ago. "Wait—why do I need the sheriff?"

The cat tipped his head to my right.

I glanced over. Macy Mulligan lay under the covers beside me with an enormous silver sword sticking out of her chest. Her unseeing eyes stared straight upward, dead.

The cat shrugged. "Don't look at me; *I* didn't kill her."

I threw my head back and screamed.

STOCK 'ER UP, BOYS!

he tall, pointy-bearded sheriff marched into Macy's tent minutes after I discovered her body, accompanied by what appeared to be two hulking trolls.

"Sheriff Watson Boswell. Friend to the law-abiding, but yer worst enemy be ye a criminal." He planted his hands on his hips and glared at the enormous sword sticking out of Macy's chest. I stood close to the tent flaps nibbling my thumb, while Mort—the cat—sat beside me.

The sheriff wore a fancy doublet with gold buttons down the middle, a leather hat with a huge feather, and puffy pantaloons tucked into his cuffed leather boots. Pretty fancy duds for a sheriff. Ol' Watson might be more friendly to the "rich and donating" than anything else.

He scratched his bearded chin, thought it over all

of two seconds, then pointed a thick, ring-encrusted finger at me. "She did it. Arrest her!"

Despite my protests of innocence, I soon found myself locked in the pillory for the entire morning with a wooden sign hung round my neck that read: Naughty. Seemed kind of an understatement considering the charges, but maybe the sheriff didn't have a readymade one for "cold-blooded killer."

The first couple of hours weren't so bad. One of the benefits of being barely over five feet was that I didn't have to bend forward as much as a taller person would have. It made having my head and wrists clamped between two big boards of wood *slightly* less uncomfortable.

But it was nearly noon now, according to the big clock tower across the square, and the tipsy Fairegoers had discovered it was fun to throw things at my head—which was apparently something you could pay the sheriff to do.

What a racket. Plus, the sun was beating down so hot, I had sweat tickling my hairline. Speaking of which…

"Mort, could you scratch my cheek? It itches."

Macy's black cat seemed to have adopted me as his new owner. He'd followed me out to the stocks and hung around all morning—though the mice were still nowhere to be seen.

Suspish, Mort. Suspish.

The cat sat in the tiny sliver of shade directly

beneath the stocks. "Would that I could, but alas, I do not wish to become a target."

As if on cue, a tomato hurtled toward my head. I squeezed my eyes shut, waiting for the impact, but it splattered against the wood beside me, spraying my cheek with particulate.

I smirked at the middle-aged man in Birkenstocks who'd chucked it. "Missed me!"

He scowled and conferred with one of the sheriff's trolls.

Mort flopped down on his side, the tip of his tail whipping the dirt. "Dost thou never learn? Taunting only makes the peasants throw *more* things."

Oh, I'd learned. But at this point my back ached, my scalp had a sunburn, I was parched and starving, and I felt pretty sure my next stop was the guillotine or the hangman's noose or whatever vigilante justice they meted out here at this insane Faire. What did I have to lose?

I'd already tried screaming for help, insisting I was being held here against my will. But everyone either ignored me or chuckled, as if it was all part of the act. I had to give it to these crazy Ren Faire carnies—it was a brilliant cover.

"'Scuse me, miss?"

I strained to turn my head. A buxom blond who looked about my age—early thirties—stood nearby in a corset and long dress holding a couple of tankards and turkey legs. Pretty milkmaids' braids framed her round face, and her friendly smile faltered, which gave me just enough warning to squeeze my eyes shut.

SMASH!

A water balloon hit me square on the cheek and drenched my face. I shot the guy in Birkenstocks a flat look, my cheek stinging.

His preteen son high-fived him. "Nice shot, Dad!"

So glad I could be of service in this beautiful moment of family bonding. The family wandered off, and the troll meandered back to the jail. At last— a bit of reprieve.

The blond crouched down to my eye level. "Mind if I join you, miss?"

I raised an incredulous brow. Who would want to join me?

She pulled a roughly hewn stool over and settled herself in front of me. Carefully, she set the foaming tankards on the grassy lawn, then held one juicy, delicious-smelling leg up in front of me.

Was this some new form of torture the sheriff had devised? Tempting me with enormous portions of food and then withholding them?

But the blond gave me a sweet smile. "Thought you might be hungry?" Her English accent came out in a singsong cadence.

I meant to laugh, but it came out as a whimper. "Starving."

Mort rolled toward her and lifted a paw. "I, as well."

She seemed completely unfazed by the talking cat and bent forward to scratch between his ears. "You poor dear."

She ripped off a piece of turkey and gave it to Mort. She then held the leg directly up to my face. It wasn't the most dignified thing in the world, but I ripped off a hunk with my teeth and closed my eyes in bliss as I chewed.

"Oh, yum."

She shot me a pitying look. "Sorry everyone's throwing bladders of water at your head."

I shrugged my aching shoulders. "It's okay. It's so hot out here, it's actually refreshing."

"I'm Hilde." She held up the turkey leg for me to take another bite, while she munched on her own.

I spoke around my bite. "I'm Adelaide. Call me Laidey, though."

Hilde's big blue eyes grew round. "Lady?" She folded forward in a deep bow. "Oh, m'lady, what an injustice they've done to you! I offer myself as your humble servant."

"What? Oh." I flapped my hand in an attempt to wave her off. "It's just a nickname. I'm not an actual lady."

But Hilde shook her head, hands clasped at her ample chest. "Oh m'lady, I shall do my best to free you."

I thought about protesting more but didn't have the energy. Instead, I just ripped off another bite of the turkey leg. After I chewed and swallowed, she did her best to tip some beer from the tankard into my mouth. Most ended up dribbling down my chin and throat, but the one gulp of ice-cold liquid I got was worth it.

I frowned at Hilde as she sipped from her own tankard. "Why are you helping me?" Nobody else had.

She shrugged. "Ah, well, I can't stand to see someone sufferin', you know." She handed Mort another piece of turkey. "Besides, I figure once you're let out of there, if ye aren't hanged, it'd be best to be friends with the cold-blooded killer—not on her bad side."

"I didn't kill Macy Mulligan!"

"Of course not, m'lady." Hilde struggled to wink.

I shook my head. "For real. I just got here, I don't know anyone—why would I kill her?"

"I wouldn't blame ye if ye did." She flashed her eyes. "*Nobody* liked her. Plus, if ye hadn't killed her, yeh'd have ended up like Lavinia."

"Truer words ne'er spoken," Mort chimed in. He rose up on his hind legs and placed his little paws on Hilde's skirt. She fed him another piece of turkey leg.

"Who's Lavinia?"

Mort blinked his bright green eyes at me. "Macy's

former indentured servant. She slaved away for three decades before earning her freedom."

"Yeesh." My stomach turned. Macy had been eager to "claim me," as she'd put it, and had clearly planned to put me to work. Maybe I should be grateful to whoever killed her. Then again, I wasn't sure "locked in the stocks" was a huge upgrade from indentured servant.

Hilde shook her head, her gaze wistful. "I admire your boldness, m'lady, slaying your captor and strikin' out on your own like that. I've been with the Faire since the beginning, and I'm still only a turkey leg wench."

She held up the enormous hunk of bird. "I'd love to claim my place in the Faire one day, as a ticket seller or maybe even a shop girl. Show 'em what I'm capable of... but..." She heaved a great sigh. "But I should keep my feet on the ground and head out of the clouds, as my pa always said. I'm probably only good for dishin' poultry and fillin' draughts."

I frowned. I might not have taught a Pilates class in months, but the instincts to encourage and motivate were deep in me. I'd heard clients belittle themselves for their perceived weakness, lack of coordination, and hundreds more shortcomings. I'd never been okay with standing by while people talked so badly of themselves, and I wasn't about to start now.

"Hilde."

She and Mort looked up at me.

"That's not true." With my wrist clamped between the stocks, I did my best to lift my palm. "I may have just met you, but I know that you're incredibly kind and generous—just look how you're taking care of Mort and me."

Hilde's fair cheeks blushed bright pink, and she looked down at her lap.

"And I know you're brave. No one else dared approach a suspected murderer."

This got a small smile out of her.

I decided to capitalize on her misunderstanding. "I hereby order you to stop speaking so badly of yourself. Agreed?"

She grinned up at me. "Yes, m'lady."

I grinned back. "Good."

Sheriff Watson Boswell and his troll constables exited the jail and marched straight over to us. Oh goody.

Hilde leaped to her feet and bowed her head, while Mort log rolled behind my ankles.

I sighed at the lawmen. "What now?"

The sheriff glared at me. "Your bail has been paid, Adelaide Ryan." He jerked his chin at a leering troll, who stomped forward with a big iron ring of keys and unlocked the stocks.

Was this a heat-stroke-induced hallucination? Warily I straightened, though my spine wouldn't quite cooperate. *Oof.* I'd need to do some stretches, stat. I rubbed my sore wrists and peered up at the sheriff.

"Who bailed me out?" I looked at Hilde, but she shook her head.

The sheriff crossed his arms over his barrel chest. "He wished to remain anonymous."

I smirked. "So it's a 'he.'"

"Blast!" He bared his teeth. "Fine, you know that much. But the rest is a secret." He pointed a ring-covered finger at me. "Thou art hereby released on the condition that you don't go far, though." He smirked and his trolls giggled like hyenas.

"Right." I pressed my lips together. "Because I'm trapped here. Good one."

The sheriff stalked closer, and I crinkled my nose at his heavy stench of sweat and stale pipe tobacco. "Yer trial's set for four days from now. Earliest we figured the queen might've slept off her hangover, may she die before her time." He grinned maliciously. "Enjoy yer last days. I'll have you hanging in the noose soon enough."

It seemed they hadn't heard of "presumed innocent" here. I gulped but attempted to square my throbbing shoulders. He shot me one last hard look, then spun on his booted heel and stomped back to the jail with his trolls close behind.

"Hoo!" Hilde eyed me with awe, her hands clasped under her chin. "Goodness, m'lady, you *are* fearless!"

My legs wobbled beneath me, but I was glad I'd *appeared* fearless, at least. I collapsed onto the wooden stool Hilde had brought over, and Mort slinked between my ankles.

My life might've been turned upside down, but no way was I hanging for a crime I didn't commit. I wouldn't give ol' Sherriff Boswell the pleasure.

I gratefully took a swig of the grog Hilde offered me, then wiped the foam from my lips with the back of my hand. "I'm going to figure out who really did kill Macy Mulligan and prove my innocence, or die trying."

"Me-*yow*." Mort winked.

THE FAIRE

*A*fter I polished off the rest of my turkey leg and beer tankard (which took about three minutes), Hilde, Mort, and I headed back to the gates. After confirming that indeed, a magical force field prevented me from leaving (which took me several full-speed sprints headfirst into said barrier) we strolled through the Faire.

It all looked so different than it had yesterday. For one, I wasn't trying to drown out my date's constant factoids about the airspeed velocity of African sparrows or whatnot.

For another thing, I now realized that aside from the human visitors, everyone else here was actual supernatural beings. The fairies were fairies, the elves were actual elves and—holy moly—were the knights actually jousting in earnest? Aside from the horror of being trapped here forever, it was actually pretty magical.

We strolled by a giant fishbowl with shimmering mermaids swimming in loop the loops. I shook my head. "I'm not even sure where to start."

Hilde sucked on her lips and nodded thoughtfully. "Well, m'lady, we best be findin' you a place to stay." She raised her blonde brows at me. "That tent is fair bloody, so ye can't be going back to the murder scene."

I cringed. *No, thank you.* "Speaking of the murder..." While I saw the wisdom in securing a place to sleep, I'd been thinking more along the lines of how to go about discovering the killer to prove my innocence. I wanted to ask Hilde more about something she'd mentioned earlier.

"That former indentured servant of Macy's... what was her name again? Do you think she might've been angry enough to kill?"

"Oh, Lavinia?" Hilde nodded. "I could see it."

"Undoubtedly," Mort agreed. "But doth it not seem more likely that Lavinia would have killed her sometime in the three decades she'd been in servitude? Why wouldst she wait till she'd earned her freedom to risk it by murdering Macy?"

The cat had a good point. I chewed on my lip. "Who else disliked Macy?"

Hilde threw up her hands. "Oh my stars, just about everybody."

Hmph. That wasn't going to help me narrow it down. "Anyone specifically who'd want to kill her, though?"

"That's easy." Hilde leaned closer. The mouthwatering aroma of roasting turkey legs seemed cooked into her hair and clothes. Despite having eaten enough lunch to feed a small town, my stomach grumbled again. "Rumor has it Bo Erikson of the Viking Clan killed her."

I shook myself. "Wait, what?"

Mort nodded. "'Twas was one of the Viking Clan's swords embedded in Macy's chest, so that maketh sense."

I gaped. "Wait, so everyone knows about this? Why isn't the sheriff looking into it?"

Hilde and Mort exchanged guffaws.

"Because he is as corrupt as he is lazy," Mort quipped.

Great. If the law wasn't going to investigate, it was all up to me to find the killer and clear my name so I didn't end up swinging in a noose.

I turned to Hilde. "Where do the Vikings hang out?"

"At the pub, after close, most evenin's."

I nodded. Then that's where I'd be tonight, too.

"Before we get lost seeking justice, a friendly reminder that we have a show coming up."

I glanced down at Mort, who padded along

between Hilde and me, his long tail in the air. "What?"

He looked up and blinked. "Thou hast inherited me, which means thou hast inherited Macy's act." His whiskers twitched. "I suppose it will be difficult without the mice, though."

I quirked a brow. "What kind of act was this, exactly?"

Mort shook his head. "Slapstick comedy, littered with puns and innuendos—lowbrow stuff, but the crowd ate it up. While Macy quipped away, the mice would ride around on mine head like I wast their pony. They wouldst walk on tight ropes and I wouldst jump through rings of fire."

I gawked. "Sounds like you and the mice were the stars of the show."

Mort nodded. "I shall not argue thou on that, but Macy didst all the talking." He tipped his black nose in the air and shot me a significant look. "That shall be your job now."

I shook my head. "No way. Nuh-uh. I have horrible stage fright." Flashbacks of throwing up on my shirt out of nerves during the fourth-grade spelling bee flickered through my mind. Somehow, it'd always been different leading a Pilates class. Maybe it was because I felt in my element, or because class sizes were small. But I shuddered just thinking about stepping on stage at the Renaissance Faire... in front of a big crowd...

I gulped. The enormous turkey leg began to work its way back up from my stomach.

Hilde eyed me with concern, then pulled her lips to the side. "So the show's out. Well, lady or not, you wilst need a job. The royal court's all full, unfortunately, though if you ask me, I'd say stay clear of the queen's entourage."

"May she die before her time," Mort and Hilde muttered in tandem.

I shot them confused looks as we ducked around the pickle cart.

Mort explained. "The royal court is doubly cursed—they're trapped here *and* they're immortal. The rest of us just live a long time but, try as they may, there is no way out for the royals."

Hilde nodded. "The queen's tried. That's why we all wish her a speedy exit."

I nodded but didn't understand in the least. This place was bizarre.

Hilde led the way past the flower crown cart, the ribbons fluttering in the breeze. "Do you have any special talents?"

I shrugged and half-joked, "I can teach Pilates." Pretty sure they didn't have that at the Ren Faire.

Hilde frowned, her brows pinched together in confusion. "What's that?"

I lifted a palm. Feeling was slowly returning to my hands after my turn in the pillory. "It's a type of exercise class."

41

Hilde's eyes grew wide. "Oh. You were like the slave drummer then? Who keeps time on the boats for the captive rowers?"

I chuckled. "Some of my clients would probably agree with that, but no. People sign up for the class voluntarily—they pay for it, even."

"My stars." Hilde shook her head. "You must've been a mighty rich lady. Imagine—a land where food is so plentiful the peasants pay to expend energy."

I cleared my throat. "So... I guess that's out. What kind of jobs *could* I do around here?"

She scrunched up her face. "Are you good with horses? They always need help in the stables."

I winced. "No. I think they're beautiful, but I'm allergic."

Mort nodded. "I am also allergic to work."

I shot him a flat look. "Not what I meant."

"What kind of powers do you have?"

I scoffed. "To be honest, I have no idea. I didn't even know I had magic until I got trapped yesterday evening." I was still coming to terms with that part. I'd believe it when I saw it.

I'd witnessed Macy perform magic and had had conversations with a talking cat. Magic, I was convinced of. But *me* having magic? That was another thing.

"Oh, I'm sure you'll figure it out soon enough." Hilde hung her head as we meandered down a shaded lane, lined with an ocarina cart and a clothing shop.

I gave her a little nudge with my elbow. "Hey— what's wrong?"

She let out a heavy sigh. "Oh... it's just... I've been here with the Faire since the beginning, and I still don't know what my special powers are. Everyone else is a troll, or fairy, or vampire, or shifter, or witch. But after all this time, I still don't know where I belong." She bit her full bottom lip and said in a small voice, "Sometimes I'm not sure I belong here at all."

"Hey." I grabbed her hand and gave it a little shake till she looked up at me. "To be honest, I think not belonging here might be a mark in your favor."

She gave me a small grin.

"But you wouldn't be here if you didn't have a special power, right?"

"I suppose."

I locked eyes with Hilde and nodded. "You helped me out today, in a huge way. I'm going to help you figure out what your special power is, okay?"

She flashed me a bright smile and dropped to one knee. She clutched my hand and peppered the back of it with kisses. "Oh m'lady, I pledge you my allegiance till the end of days and—"

A sunburnt group of bros with tank top arm holes down to their waists whistled as they walked by.

"Okay." I yanked her to her feet and pulled my hand back. I shook my head. "We're friends, alright? No more kneeling or pledging or anything like that. Agreed?"

"Yes, m'lady." She dropped into a curtsy.

"This shall take some time." Mort snaked between my ankles.

"Oh!" Hilde looked up and clapped her hands. "I've got it! Tom needs a new apprentice."

Mort nodded his approval. "Good idea."

I raised a brow. "A true apprentice? Not an indentured servant?" I did not want to end up in another Macy Mulligan situation.

"Nope, a true apprentice." She leaned in, conspiratorially. "The last one ran off with a squire." She raised her brows, waiting for my reaction.

"Oh... right. Crazy."

Hilde nodded. "Tom only takes on clever ones, and you seem mighty clever to me, m'lady." In the distance, the clock tower struck one o'clock.

"Oh, bother! I've got to get back to the turkey leg stand. Come now, let's hurry. This way, this way!" Hilde bounded along with me and Mort in tow.

"Apprentice for what?" I called up to her over the din of drums and bagpipes. Sounded like the Scottish clan was marching nearby.

I didn't get an answer until Hilde dragged me to a stop in front of a two-story shop with leaded glass windows and a thatched roof. She swept her arm out in front of her. "Welcome to Tom's shop!"

A wooden sign shaped like a broom read:

Swept Away: Artisan Brooms.

SWEPT AWAY

*T*he rounded green door to Swept Away stood propped open by a cast iron gnome. "Tom?" Hilde called as she dashed inside.

I sucked in a little breath as I followed. "Wow."

Brooms of all sizes, shapes, and colors covered every square inch of the tall, cottage-like shop. To my left, a stone fireplace rose to the double-high ceiling, with a wood staircase winding up to the second story behind it. A broom with a twisty stick handle and wispy bristles hung sideways over the mantle, while a dozen small hand brooms hung from leather cords and ribbons around the hearth.

I tipped my head back and gaped, open-mouthed, at the plethora of brooms stuffed into the rafters overhead. They lay sideways, their bristles exploding out like they'd been shocked by light-ning. Still more brooms hung mounted on the white plaster walls, while others stood upside down, their handles stuffed into buckets and barrels.

To my right, the leaded glass windows onto the lane had been thrown open, letting in a refreshing breeze. A display of especially "artisan" brooms stood against that wall. Each had double handles, all twisted together, the bristles of the twin brooms interwoven as well. I gulped. Who knew brooms were such big business?

Then again, the shop was empty of customers so... maybe not?

"M'lady?"

Hilde's voice jolted me out of my awe. I blinked and found her standing beside a tall counter and a tiny old woman who sat perched on a stool behind it.

"M'lady, this is Tom. Tom, m'lady Adelaide. M'lady's here for the apprentice job."

I blinked in surprise. So Tom was a woman?

Hilde curtsied and winced. "Sorry, but I've got to be getting back to the turkey leg booth."

She hiked up her long skirts and scampered past me toward the door.

I looked after my one and only friend in the Faire —save the talking cat—with rising panic. "I'll see you later?" *Please!*

"Of course!" Hilde shot me a warm smile and waved before ducking outside and then sprinting past the windows. I wanted to beg her not to leave me alone.

"Well—you gonna just stand there or what?" The ancient, spindly old woman raised a faint brow.

"Oh! Sorry." I approached the broad counter.

In addition to the ledger book, feathered quill, ink pot, and a bag of cash—no doubt for ringing up sales—the counter was also littered with broom parts. Golden straw, some loose and some gathered into one-inch-wide bundles, covered the table. An assortment of tools sat beside her left hand—spools of twine in a variety of colors, silver shears, giant needles, and—*gulp*—several sharp-looking knives.

The old woman studied me for a long moment from behind her round, wire-rimmed spectacles. She wore her long white hair in twin braids over her shoulders and leaned her chin into her hand. She tapped a finger thoughtfully against her cheek, then seemed to make up her mind about something.

She hopped off her stool and came around the counter to stand in front of me. At barely five foot one, I was used to being the shortest person in the room, so I was shocked to find this little old lady only came up to my ears!

She shot a thin, though toned, arm out and shook my hand—*firmly*.

"Name's Thomasina Broomitch, but everyone just calls me Tom."

I grinned. Despite my nerves, I couldn't help but

like her straightforward manners. "I'm Adelaide Ryan, but everyone calls me Laidey."

Tom smirked. "So that's why Hilde thinks you're a lady?"

I chuckled. "Yeah. I'm definitely no noblewoman. Just a regular girl from Minneapolis. I tried to correct her but—"

Tom ignored me and crouched down to address my new black cat. "Hey, Mort. Heard about Macy. How's it feel to have your freedom?"

My cat threaded back and forth in front of the old woman as she stroked his back and tail. "It appears I am *hers* now. But I think it is an improvement."

I raised a brow. I sure hoped I was an improvement over the crazy witch who'd kept Mort locked in a cage without food or water!

Tom looked up at me, placed a hand on her thigh, and stood with a small grunt. It was the only indication so far that she might actually be as old as she looked.

"You don't plan to continue with the Cat and Mouse Show?"

I shook my head. "No. Not my thing at all." Besides, the mice were conspicuously missing. I shot my cat a doubtful look.

Tom planted her hands on her narrow hips. "So now you want to be a broom squire?"

"A what now?"

She rolled her eyes and pulled her glasses from her nose to let them hang from the beaded string around her neck. "Kids these days." She lifted a tiny, calloused palm. "A broom squire, otherwise known as a broom maker." She arched a thin brow. "Isn't that what you're here for—the job?"

I nodded. "I'd like a job, yes. Just... to be honest, I didn't even know broom maker was a job before about five minutes ago."

Tom pinched the bridge of her nose and groaned. She collected herself and tried again. "Alright, then. What kind are you?" She looked me up and down and leaned to the side to check out my back. "Don't see any wings."

I shook my head. This had to be the weirdest job interview I'd ever had. "No wings. I, uh—didn't actually know I had magic until I got trapped here yesterday."

"Hoo boy." Tom lifted her eyes to the raftered ceiling stuffed with brooms, then looked back at me. "Look kid, you have any training? Any skills at all?"

I licked my lips. While making brooms was hardly my life's dream, it seemed that I was stuck at the Faire for the time being and that I'd need a job if I wanted to survive. Compared to getting up on stage in front of a crowd (the turkey leg started to come up just thinking about it) or mucking horse stalls, working in this cute little shop with this peppy old lady seemed like a great option. Besides, even in my normal, non-magical life, it'd been months since I sold my Pilates studio. It was time to move on and try something new.

I squared my shoulders and composed myself. "I actually have experience as a small business owner myself. I can keep books, do marketing, manage payroll."

Tom arched a brow. "You actually enjoy that stuff?"

My shoulders slumped. "No." I hated it, in fact.

Mort batted at the springy bristles of a nearby broom with his little paw.

"What kind of business did you run?"

"A Pilates studio." I bit my lip when I remembered that no one here seemed to know what that was. "It's a form of exercise that—"

Tom waved me off. "I know what it is. I do yoga every morning with the council." She pointed at me. "You should join us."

"Oh, um—" It was refreshing that she actually knew what I did and oddly modern of her. Maybe she wasn't as "Renaissancey" as her dark green hooded cloak and long skirts made her appear. "Thanks."

"You *teach* Pilates too?"

"I used to." I shook my head. "Once I opened my own place, I didn't get to be on the floor as much as I liked."

Tom nodded and looked me over. "You apprentice to become an instructor, don't you?"

I nodded. "I trained under my mentor for over a year and a half."

Tom grinned. "Alright, we're onto something. Means you're good at committing, taking instruction, and have to be at least somewhat coordinated." She pointed at me. "I don't need a bookkeeper, I need a broom maker. You okay working with your hands?"

I sighed with relief and couldn't hold back a huge grin. "Yes!"

I was so ready to be done with crunching numbers and staring at a computer screen all day. Though, lately, it'd been the TV screen. I looked around the olde shoppe and realized that here at the Renaissance Faire, there were likely to be no screens at all.

I pulled my phone from my pocket and found it dead. I doubted they had extra chargers here... much less electricity. It'd take some getting used to for sure, but part of me was excited to live a little more simply, for however long I was trapped here.

"Right." Tom nodded. "We'll start you off with a trial period before I formally take you on as an apprentice. You'll need to prove you've got what it takes. Also, I want to make sure you're not the murderer everyone's saying you are."

I opened my mouth to protest, but Tom waved me off.

"I don't think you did it, just to be clear, but I figure it's best to be sure before committing to years of training."

I raised my brows. "Years?" How much training did you need to make a flippin' broom?

"Let me show you around real quick. I'll start you on the floor in sales. The more you talk about our brooms to customers, the more you'll learn about them yourself."

"Right." I wished I had something to take notes with. Mort padded along beside me, joining in on the tour.

Tom led the way around the store, pointing right, left, and overhead. "At Swept Away we sell brooms to the visitors *and* the Rennies."

I jogged to keep up with her.

She glanced back and smirked. "The tourists obviously get our standard, non-enchanted models, while the Rennies are usually looking for bespelled ones."

Did she expect me to learn how to do spells? I'd thought broom squire would be an easy job—clearly I was in over my head already.

Tom walked to the twisted, dual-handle artisan brooms beside the windows. "We've got our wedding brooms, to seal and bless a marriage." She pointed overhead to the brooms in the rafters. "We've got kitchen brooms—they're drying prior to being sewn flat. We spell some to magically do the sweeping for you—our most popular model among the Rennies."

I grinned. The original Roombas.

Tom smirked and waved me closer, lowering her voice, though no one else was around. "If you don't like a customer, sell 'em one that always leaves a tiny trickle of dirt outside the pan, no matter how many times they sweep." She cackled. "Drives 'em nuts!"

I flashed my eyes at Mort. That was downright diabolical.

Tom gestured to a broom hanging sideways over the door with a spray of feathery stalks. "We've got brooms enchanted for protection. You hang those over the door or the fireplace, if you're a witch." She stopped to look me over. "I'm thinking that's probably what you are. Most non-obvious types are witches."

I blinked. Wow. A witch, huh? Would've been handy to know that earlier—could've hexed Chad.

She pressed a tiny hand to her flat chest. "I'm a witch myself." She switched gears right back to the broom tour. "We've got cleansing brooms—they're enchanted to sweep away bad luck, illness, that sort of thing." She stopped beside a barrel of twisty-handled brooms with long bristles that formed a narrow cylinder. "These are besoms, or traditional flying brooms—that's self-explanatory."

My head swam. Could you actually fly on brooms? Was this woman pulling my leg?

"Well, there's tons more obviously, but that'll get you going." Tom spun around and looked me up and down, from my tee to my jeans to my red canvas sneakers. "I think my last apprentice left some robes and dresses behind; she was about your size." She frowned down at my feet. "We'll have to do something about those shoes, though. We can talk to the cobbler later."

I raised my brows. "Wait—I can't just wear this?"

Mort snorted, and Tom rolled her eyes. "You work at the Renaissance Faire now, what do you think? We've got to be in full costume. The visitors love it." She frowned. "Besides, you've got blood on your pants."

I glanced down and shuddered. Ew. She was right. That must be Macy's.

Tom snapped her fingers, and in the blink of an eye, a folded stack of purple velvet garments appeared in her arms. She shoved them at me. "Go get changed upstairs. First door on the right—that'll be your bedroom."

Hope surged through me. "I have a bedroom?" Fingers crossed it included a bed made of something other than straw.

Tom nodded. "Room and an allowance for board is included in the apprenticeship."

I grinned. Maybe my standards had lowered after

being abducted by Macy last night and enduring her hovel of a tent, but it looked like things were looking up for ol' Laidey!

Tom bent forward and cooed at Mort. "And lucky for you, pets are allowed."

He bounded over to the stairs. "I calleth foot of the bed!"

I grinned as Tom ushered me to get changed. "Hurry back down when you're done—you're on sales, starting now."

By the time the Faire closed, it was clear I was the world's worst salesperson. Sure, I'd sold new clients on the benefits of Pilates, but that was something I was passionate about.

But brooms? I knew nothing about brooms. I hadn't even owned a broom since... ever! In fact, during the darkest days of my post-Chad depression, one of my hobbies had been feeding cheese noodles to my Roomba.

Tom gaped at me from her perch on the stool. "You're a disaster!" She sounded more awed than angry.

I winced, and even my new enchanted cat shook his head. "What *was* that? Earlier, thou rode a broom around like a bucking bronco... in front of a family."

I grimaced. "I was trying to get a laugh out of the kids." I shook my sweaty palms. "I don't know! I'm sorry. Urg." I paced between racks of brooms. "I have stage fright, and I guess that felt like performing and I panicked!"

Mort scoffed, and Tom watched with wide blue eyes. "Clearly."

My shoulders slumped. My purple velvet skirts with the leather corset were stifling in the muggy summer heat. My feet hurt, I was hungry, I was about to be fired, and oh yeah—I was cursed to spend eternity in the Faire, if I wasn't hanged for murder. Not a great first day.

Tom dragged her hands down her wrinkled face. "Your talents do not lie in sales." She groaned. "We'll have to figure something else out."

I bit my lip, feeling a little glimmer of hope. Maybe she hadn't entirely given up on me yet. She untied her little money pouch and flipped me a heavy gold coin.

"Get yourself something to eat, and don't stay out too late. We're up at dawn tomorrow."

"Right—yoga." My stomach twisted with guilt as I gazed at the coin in my palm. I certainly hadn't earned it. In fact, I'd probably—no, *definitely*—cost Tom customers. I cringed as I remembered when I'd demonstrated how lovely the brooms were to sweep with and accidentally poked that guy in the eye with the stick end.

I glanced up as Thomasina tromped upstairs. "I'll

be up bright and early!" I called after her. "Tomorrow, I'll do better. I won't let you down!"

Even I didn't believe that.

Mort and I stepped out into the mostly empty lane. Crickets chirped as the sun dipped further below the horizon and the sky grew inky. Lights flickered on in windows above closed shops, and the hint of singing wafted over the breeze. Must be the nightly song at the gates. I wondered if anyone else had gotten trapped.

Mort licked his lips. "I recommend the fish and chips."

I shot him a little grin. "Sounds good, but we have a job to do first. We need to check out that Viking, Bo Erikson. The one whose sword ended up in Macy's chest." I raised a brow. "Do you know where that pub Hilde mentioned is?"

Mort sighed but lifted his tail. "Follow me."

We passed a tall, elegant couple with slightly pointed ears. They whispered behind their hands and moved to the other side of the street to avoid me. A couple of ogres and some noblemen did the same.

It was hot and humid, and I hadn't showered in over twenty-four hours. I probably wasn't smelling like a rose, but what gave?

The tip of Mort's tail twitched side to side. "They think you killed Macy, remember?"

He ducked down a narrow alleyway littered with

crates and empty pallets. I hiked up my skirts and picked my way between them. "Seriously? Everyone thinks *I* did it?"

Mort glanced back, his green eyes glowing in the shadows. "Thou art new, for one. Plus, word travels fast. I'd wager the whole Faire heard about Macy and your arrest ere the sheriff even threw you in the pillory."

I heaved a great sigh. "Fantastic." Looked like I wouldn't be making many friends until I cleared my name.

Mort led the way toward the sign that read Wilde's Abbey.

Huh. I'd passed by here last night with Macy. She'd told a Viking dude that she'd be stopping by later. Was it just a coincidence that she'd then been killed with a Viking sword?

I gulped and held the heavy wooden door open for Mort, then ducked inside. It took my eyes a moment to adjust to the mood lighting. A fire crackled in the massive stone fireplace despite the summer heat, and candles flickered from iron chandeliers that hung from the raftered ceiling. A trio of a fiddler, flutist, and drummer played lively Irish music on a small wooden stage. The upbeat tunes were barely audible over the raucous laughter and chatter from the absolutely packed tables.

I hoped to see if anything had happened between the Vikings and Macy last night but wasn't ready to march up to the long table of burly men and start interrogating them. Mort and I threaded between tables of tall, slender elves, bearded dwarves, fairies with glittering wings, and pirates. I didn't spot the handsome captain from yesterday, though.

I slid onto one of the few empty stools at the bar, and Mort leapt gracefully onto the one beside me. I leaned my elbows on the aged wooden bar top and glanced around. "Wow. This place fills up fast!"

Mort lifted his tiny cat chin and peered up over the bar toward the rows of glass bottles—some of them glowing. "Raquel hath a great selection of draughts." He winked at me. "Plus she poureth with a heavy hand."

Nice. I could use a stiff drink after the last two days.

A well-endowed woman, probably in her early forties, slid down the bar as she polished a silver tankard. "Hiya, honey. What can I get you and your furry friend?" She winked at my cat. "Hey, Mort."

He meowed back.

I sat taller in my seat and adjusted my corset. I was positive that I was not wearing mine as well as she was hers. Auburn curls tumbled from the pile on top of her head to frame her pretty face as she waited for my answer.

"Uh... what's good here?"

She sniffed. "You must be new. It's all good here. Devilishly good." Her dark eyes twinkled with the flames from the fireplace. "I'm Raquel Wilde—this is my place."

I shot her a nervous smile. This woman commanded respect, and I had the distinct sense I didn't want to get on her bad side. "Laidey Ryan."

"Hi, Laidey. Welcome to the Faire. First round's on me." She spun to face the back wall, her long skirt twirling around her legs. She filled up a chilled metal tankard with foaming beer, then slid it across the bar to me.

"Thank you." I was tempted to lean my sweaty forehead against the deliciously ice-cold mug.

She crouched down, her cleavage threatening to spill out, then rose with a dish of milk and set it on the bar in front of my cat. I grinned as Mort placed his paws on the bar and eagerly lapped it up.

Raquel turned to go, but I reached out. "Um—sorry, but do you know Bo Erikson?"

She grinned and jerked her chin behind me. "Can't miss him."

She hurried off to take another order and I spun on my stool.

A burly blond guy the size of a refrigerator stood with a bear pelt slung around his shoulders and a metal helmet perched atop his head, twin horns curling toward the sky. He hugged a scrawny young man to his side.

"Hear, hear for young Bo Erikson!" His booming voice cut through the din of the tavern.

The table of Vikings stomped their feet and banged their tankards on the table in a deafening uproar.

Bo gave a faltering smile, his shoulders squeezed up to his ears in what must've been a crushing side hug. He looked more like a computer nerd than a Viking to me.

"He's proved himself worthy of the Viking Clan! Skol!"

The Vikings all raised their tankards and mugs and shouted "Skol!"

Proved himself? Were they referring to him killing Macy? Was this like a gang initiation? I noted that all the Vikings up and down the table wore swords at their hips or had lain them on the table in front of them... except for Bo.

Mort and I nursed our drinks as I mulled over various ways to pull the guy aside for a word. The opportunity literally came to me.

Bo sidled up to the empty spot at the bar to my left. Leather straps crisscrossed his skinny bare chest, and a notably empty scabbard hung at his hip. He set a leather pouch down with a *clink* on the bar, then drummed his fingers as he waited for Raquel.

This was my chance! I put on my friendliest smile. "I couldn't help but overhear that toast. Impressive."

He smirked, the tiniest hint of sparse stubble

covering his chin. Man, was he even old enough to legally drink?

"Thanks. I'm Bo Erikson."

"Adelaide Ryan."

Recognition flashed across his eyes, and his cocky attitude turned immediately cagey. "Ur. Hey."

So he'd heard the rumors about me. Maybe I could use that to my advantage.

I twirled a finger toward the table of Vikings. "You must've done something pretty brave to earn those guys' respect."

His eyes widened behind his glasses. "Oh, uh— just a Viking initiation thing."

I found myself doubting, more than ever, that this nervous, scrawny kid was capable of murdering in cold blood. "Word on the street is you killed Macy Mulligan."

He looked like a deer in the headlights, so I hurried to add, "Don't know if you heard, but she 'claimed' me and was going to use me as her slave." I sniffed. "Seems like I owe you one."

His fear morphed into bravado. "Oh, uh—yeah, that's right. I did kill that old wench."

Seriously, why was every woman at the Faire a *wench*? I pushed past it. "Is that why you're missing your sword?" I looked down at his empty scabbard.

"Er… yeahhh."

This kid was a terrible liar. I decided to test him. "How'd you break in?"

He shrugged, his lip curled like he was too cool for school. "I just kicked the door open."

I frowned. "Don't you mean tent flap?"

"Er… yeah. Totally."

I shot him a puzzled look. "Didn't Macy fight back at all before you lopped off her head?"

"Psh." Bo sniffed it off. "She was a witch, but she wasn't any match for me. Just whoosh!" He made a sword-swinging motion. "Cut it clean off at the neck."

Charming. And also completely fabricated. I was starting to wonder if this kid even knew who Macy Mulligan was.

"That's funny, considering she was stabbed in the chest."

The whites showed all around Bo's eyes as he let out a little squeak. "I, uh—gotta go." He spun around, but I cleared my throat.

"You forgot your money."

He snatched up the pouch and scrambled back to the Viking table, shooting me lots of nervous glances over his shoulder. I shook my head and spun back around on my stool just as Raquel wandered over.

She frowned and glanced past me toward Bo. "Didn't he want a drink?"

"I think I scared him off."

The busty lady chuckled, then leaned forward. "He's new. Got trapped just a few months ago and has been trying to prove he belongs with the Vikings ever since." She rolled her eyes. "If he killed Macy Mulligan, then I'm a saint! Boy would be no match for a witch as powerful as she. Besides, he's as forgetful as they come." She sniffed and patted the bar before moving off. "He'd have lost his own head if it weren't attached to his body."

I glanced back over my shoulder at Bo and the table of boisterous Vikings, then leaned close to Mort.

"Maybe Bo forgot his sword somewhere."

The cat narrowed his eyes. "Art thou thinking someone else found it and used it to kill Macy?"

I shrugged. "It's a good way to frame him, right? Only, he's using it to his advantage to prove he's 'tough.'"

I sighed and hunched over my mug of beer. If Bo Erikson didn't kill Macy, then who else wanted her dead? And who might've gotten ahold of Bo's sword?

DINNER

The cold mug of beer at Wilde's Abbey had done me wonders, but I was in the mood for more than just a liquid dinner. Mort and I left the tavern and meandered through the streets of the Faire in search of food. I had to admit, the mood after hours was pretty magical.

I passed the lush, treed entrance to the Enchanted Forest, and the sounds of a bubbling brook, ethereal singing, and a harp reached my ears. Golden lights spilled from the windows of homes above shops, and fireflies flitted around the base of massive trees. I frowned—at least I thought they were fireflies. The way things had been going lately, they might just as easily have been fairies.

Mort led the way with his tail in the air. "Most of the food stalls are this way."

"Aren't they closed?"

"Nay. They stayeth open for several hours after close for all of us Rennies."

Good for me, but poor Hilde—she must be working such long days at the turkey leg booth.

As we neared the food court area, it became obvious that I'd waited too long to appease my rumbling stomach. Apparently, everyone else who worked the Faire had the same idea as Mort and me. The lines in front of every stall and cart stretched back at least a dozen deep.

I groaned, then spotted one place with no line at all. "Score!"

Mort trotted along beside me as we approached Ye Olde Bowl of Bread. Unlike all the other restaurants, the tables stood nearly empty out in front, and we were able to walk right up to the order window. I hoped they were open.

I tapped my fingers on the wooden shelf and peered into the back. "Hello?" Pots and pans clanged from somewhere nearby, and the lights were on— good signs. The delicious aroma of fresh baked bread made my mouth water, and I bounced on my heels, anxious to get some food.

"Oh!" A middle-aged woman hurried up to the window, drying her hands on a kitchen towel. She looked down at me and gave me a weak smile. Curly strands of dirty blond hair escaped from her cap and clung to her damp cheeks and neck. Must be hot, cooking back in the kitchen. "Are you here to... to order?" Her soft, meek voice held a note of incredulity.

I smiled and nodded. What else would I be here to do?

Her narrow shoulders hunched, and she could barely meet my eyes. "Wh—What will you have?"

It took me a moment to figure out why she seemed so spooked. Oh yeah... my reputation as a murderer. I decided to try to meet this head on. "You must've heard the rumors about me."

She glanced up with wide eyes, then dropped her gaze back to her feet.

I put on my friendliest smile. "I'm Laidey. And I promise, I didn't kill Macy, but I *would* love to order one of your delicious-smelling bread bowls of soup."

Quite the smooth transition, there.

The woman gave a brief nod. "We've got chowder tonight. Clam or Bacon." Well, we weren't besties, but she was at least taking my order.

"Bacon, please." I handed the woman my gold coin, and she gave me back change in the form of silver coins. I'd have to learn the Faire's currency at some point.

"Just a minute." She hurried to the back room.

"Whateth about me?" Mort purred and snaked between my ankles.

I grinned down at him. "I'll share."

As I waited for the nervous woman to return with my food, I glanced around the court again.

Strings of lights and blazing torches lit the whole area in warm light. All the other food stalls were turning a booming business, and their crowded tables out front lent the space a lively atmosphere. All except in front of Ye Olde Bread Bowl. Was that a bad sign?

My gaze drifted to the two kids sitting at a picnic bench nearby. A boy and a girl, they looked like twins with their pale skin and white-blond bowl cuts. I'd guess they were about eleven—though I was a horrible judge of children's ages. *They* certainly seemed to be enjoying their soup, at least. They each clutched their bread bowls, frantically gnawing at the rims. I curled my lip. *Yikes*—their parents, wherever they were, needed to work on their manners.

"Order's up, miss."

I startled as the soft-spoken woman appeared at the window again. I thanked her and eagerly carried my bread bowl and silver spoon over to a picnic table. Mort leapt onto the bench beside me, and we inhaled the steam curling up off the thick, creamy soup. My mouth watered, and I realized that if it weren't for propriety, I'd probably devour my bread bowl like those two kids over there.

Mort purred loudly beside me as I dipped my spoon into the chunky soup and raised a bite to my lips.

"I wouldn't do that if I were you."

I snapped my mouth shut and glanced up at the

handsome pirate captain who stood across the table from me. I gulped. I'd somehow forgotten how dashing he was with that thick, black 'stache, smoldering gaze, and pirate getup. I blinked. Wait. After all I'd learned about the Faire's workers being actual kings and knights and elves, did that mean this guy truly was a pirate captain?

He shot me a friendly, heart-stopping grin and gestured at the bench across from me. "May I?"

I nodded, too flustered by his good looks and sudden appearance to speak.

He perched on the bench and leaned forward with those broad shoulders and dark, twinkling eyes. For a brief moment I hallucinated he was going to kiss me. "Friendly advice, don't eat the soup."

I blinked, then glanced down and realized I was still holding the spoon halfway to my mouth. I dropped it back into the bowl and whined. "Why? Are you here to tell me it's cursed, too?"

He flashed me a brilliant smile and chuckled. It made me a little too happy that I'd made him laugh.

"No." He raised a large hand to the side of his mouth. "But rumor has it people have found hair and mouse droppings in their food."

"Ugh!" I leaned back and shoved the bread bowl away from me.

Mort groaned.

Well, that explained all the empty tables. My stomach turned a little at the way the pale twins were nibbling away with abandon. "I just want a bite to eat, for frick's sake! Is this whole place unsafe?" I threw my hands up. "How am I supposed to know what's going on? Cursed candy, now contaminated soup?" I groaned and dropped my head into my hands.

The pirate's soft chuckling was both irritating and attractive. "You'll learn the ropes. It'll just take time—which you've got plenty of." He rose and walked around the table to my side. "C'mon."

A little tingle of excitement jolted through me as I took the warm, strong hand he extended to me.

"I'm Captain Bruce Roberts, by the by."

"Adelaide—but call me Laidey."

Bruce gently pulled me to my feet, and Mort sprang off the bench to walk beside me as we headed away from the bread bowl place.

I thought over his comment about time. Hilde had also mentioned everyone in the Faire living awhile. "How long have you been here? At the Faire, I mean?"

He gave me a tight-lipped smile. "A long while by some measures… blink of an eye, by others."

I shot him a flat look. "How mysterious of you."

He threw his head back and laughed.

I tried not to be too disappointed when Bruce dropped my hand. "Let's go get you something decent to eat." He leaned in conspiratorially. "I have an in at the gyro place—we can cut the line. This one's on me."

I grinned up at him. "Thank you, but you don't need to do that." I sighed. "You've done enough to help me already. I should've listened to your warning about that candy yesterday."

He laced his hands together behind his back as we threaded through the lines of Rennies, mouthwatering aromas scenting the air. "True, you probably should have." He cleared his throat. "But then I wouldn't have the pleasure of taking you to dinner."

My eyes widened. Was this a date? "Again, you don't have to treat me. I got paid today." It was true —the silver coins jingled in my pocket with each step.

Plus, as tall, dark, and handsome as this pirate was, I wasn't sure I was ready to jump into romance on my first day trapped in an enchanted Faire. I'd barely been ready for my date with Cliff the bird man —and look how well that had turned out. Besides, after my cheating fiancé, I'd developed a deep (and probably unfair) mistrust of good-looking men.

Bruce winked. "It's the least I can do to welcome you to the Faire. Besides, don't worry about the payment. I've got literal boatloads of treasure."

I shook my head at him, grinning. "Are you trying to impress me with your riches?"

He raised a thick brow. "Did it work?"

I shook my head. *This guy.*

He shrugged his broad shoulders. "Ah, well. Worth a try."

"So your treasures… you're really a pirate? I mean, not like Bo Erikson who joined the Faire and decided to become a Viking, or me, who's now a broom maker… sort of."

He rested his hand on the hilt of his sword like it was second nature. "Aye, I am a real pirate. Me and my whole crew sailed the seven seas before we found our way to the Faire."

Huh. So he and his whole crew got trapped here. There was clearly a story there.

"Ah, here we are." I followed him down a narrow alleyway to a wooden back door. Mice squeaked from behind a crate, and Mort's ears pricked.

"Just rodents." Bruce gave Mort and me a bracing look. "The food court takes extra precautions to keep the gnomes out."

"A pox upon them!" My cat hissed.

Okay. So gnomes—bad. Got it.

Bruce knocked on the back door, then leaned against the wall, ankles crossed.

"Aren't you worried about taking a murderer to dinner? Everyone else is." I'd tried to ignore the whispering and side-eye looks as we passed by earlier.

Captain Bruce's mustache twitched with his bright smile. "I know you did not kill anyone."

I shot him a look. "How?"

He shrugged. "Maybe it's because I've lived a long time and know a killer when I see one."

I sucked in a breath as something slid into place. Convinced of my innocence? Boatloads of treasure? Taking me to dinner? The only person I'd spoken to yesterday? Check, check, check, and check.

Bruce shot me a quizzical look.

"You paid my bail."

His cheeks flushed pink in the light from the lantern hanging beside the back door. Had I actually made a pirate captain blush?

He looked away. "'Twas nothing."

I gaped, torn between gratitude and suspicion. It was a huge thing he'd done for me—but I was also afraid of what he might expect in return. "Thank you."

He nodded and uncrossed, then recrossed his arms, still not meeting my eyes. "Don't mention it."

I drew myself up as tall as my small frame would allow me. "But, to be clear, I'm not going to be your indentured servant or whatever you kids are calling it these days."

He chuckled and looked up. "No strings attached. Did I mention I've got boatloads of treasure?"

I relaxed, convinced that he didn't want to dwell on the bail issue any more than I did. "Maybe once or twice." After Macy's "favors," I was just a little more suspicious of gifts. But if this handsome pirate wanted to spring me from the stocks and buy me a gyro, I wasn't going to argue.

The door cracked open. "What?" A tanned bald man poked his head out, then spotted Bruce and threw the door open. "Bruce!"

The big guy in the white apron threw his arms around the pirate, and they embraced. Then Bruce held up two fingers. "Two gyro plates for me and the lady, and—" He looked at Mort. "—another for the cat?"

Bruce was winning friends all over the place.

POPPY LACEWING

$\mathcal{I}$ squeezed my eyes shut and moaned around my bite of gyro. "Have I mentioned this is delicious?"

Captain Bruce flashed me one of his distractingly bright smiles from across the table. "Once or twice."

The juicy, perfectly spiced meat melted in my mouth as I stabbed a fork into some feta cheese and greek salad. For months after Chad broke it off, I'd wallowed away on my couch, subsisting on potato chips and frozen pizza. I realized now that my "comfort" food hadn't actually been all that comforting. I'd been missing out on some seriously delectable food.

I glanced around the "food court" of sorts. Elves, noblewomen, minstrels, and men and women with scarves tied round their heads crowded together at the picnic tables. Strings of lights crisscrossed overhead and illuminated the grassy space in the center of all the food stalls.

It'd been a while since I'd enjoyed a night out with other humans... and assorted creatures. Mort perched on the bench beside me, happily chowing down on his own dinner.

I took a big bite of my salad, and the tangy goat cheese mixed with the spice of red onion and crispy lettuce. "Yum. Well, if I have to be trapped in this Faire forever, at least there's good food."

Bruce lifted his pita in salute. "Amen."

I grabbed my gyro and glanced up at him over the rim of it. What was such a debonair, good-looking man treating me to dinner for? On one hand, he might just be taking pity on me. I'd been smack dab in the middle of a drunken breakdown yesterday after running into my ex and his new girl. And then today I'd spent most of the day locked in the pillory while Faire visitors chucked water balloons at my head.

I shook off any thoughts that he might have some sort of romantic interest in me. It had to be pity.

I was going in for another bite of delicious gyro meat when a small, high-pitched voice startled me.

"Oh, you would be a carnivore, wouldn't you?"

I spun to face a young woman with fluttering gossamer fairy wings on her back. I gulped and lowered my gyro with a frown.

"Sorry—do I know you?"

The fairy's pointy ears poked up through her long golden hair, and the fresh flower crown around her head belied her intimidating air. She glared her big eyes at me, glitter and jewels sparkling at their corners, and held out a dainty palm. "Hand the mice over. I know you inherited them after you killed Macy Mulligan."

I blinked at her in confusion and Bruce held up his big palms. "Come now, Poppy, I think there's been a misunderstanding—"

She stomped her tiny, bare foot and shrieked, "Hand them over!"

Diners spun to stare, and the good-natured hubbub of conversation quieted as those around us eavesdropped.

Great. Just what I needed—*more* negative attention.

I squared my shoulders and spun fully to face the petite, fuming fairy.

"First of all, I didn't kill Macy Mulligan. And secondly, I don't know where the mice are." I shot Mort a side-eye look. I mean, I had a pretty good idea of where they might be...

Poppy's chest heaved. "The cat then!" She pointed a trembling finger at Mort, who sat on the bench beside me.

The chubby black cat scoffed. "Methinks not."

The fairy stomped over to Mort. "There, there kitty," she cooed, her soft words undermined by her tense tone. She reached for him, but he hissed and swatted at her. It was the most energetic I'd seen Mort yet!

"I am my own cat, thank you." Mort's green eyes narrowed to slits as he warily watched the fairy.

Poppy lurched back with a huff.

I frowned at her, perplexed. "Why do you want Macy's animals?"

She jutted her pointed chin in the air. "Because Macy's act was inhumane! She made those poor creatures perform like circus animals."

Mort tipped his head to the side. "She doth speaketh the truth."

Poppy threw a tiny hand up. "She barely fed them enough, and she was overall just a terrible mouse and cat mother! Now hand 'em over!"

I agreed with her assessment of Macy Mulligan's pet ownership skills—or lack thereof—but my sympathy with the fairy stopped there. "In case you haven't noticed, I don't think Mort *wants* to go with you."

The fairy's glittery cheeks flushed bright red, and her wild eyes told me I was in for another tirade. Bruce rose from his seat to intervene but was saved the trouble by the approach of Sheriff Watson Boswell. He swaggered over, thumbs looped into his belt below his large belly, accompanied by his two massive troll henchmen.

Those at the tables surrounding us quickly spun

around and got back to their own business as the sheriff glowered down at Poppy, Bruce, Mort, and me.

He shot an especially condescending look my way. "Art thou causing problems again, Marmalade?"

I shot him a flat look. "It's Adelaide. And no!"

Poppy the fairy stomped her foot. "Make her give me Macy's animals!"

The sheriff groaned and pinched the bridge of his nose with a leather-gloved hand. "Not this again."

I raised my brows. "Again?" I looked between Bruce and Mort. "This is an ongoing thing?"

The sheriff scoffed. "She's been whining for weeks."

Poppy's eyes blazed as she whirled on the sheriff. Her flower crown barely reached his chest, but still, he and the trolls staggered back under the force of her fury. "Whining? I've been filing formal complaints for weeks. That woman was grossly irresponsible with her animals, and this one doesn't look much better." She threw a disdainful look my way, and I gasped.

"You don't know me!"

She ignored me and continued to chew out the sheriff and his cringing trolls. "And what have you done about it, hm?" She took a deep breath and made prayer hands at her chest. "Listen, I'm a peace-loving fairy who cares for all creatures, great and small. I'm a vegetarian and believe that love is the way." Her soft demeanor hardened in an instant. "But if you think I'm just going to stand by and let poor, innocent animals be mistreated—"

I glanced at my fat cat, Mort, and thought of the empty mouse cage. Not sure how innocent he was...

"—then you've got another think coming, because Poppy Lacewing is no pushover!" The petite fairy jabbed her finger into the retreating sheriff's chest. "Don't make me tell the fairy queen about this."

The sheriff's eyes widened before he gathered himself and scoffed, though his round eyes still held fear. "She doesn't have jurisdiction."

Poppy bared her teeth. "We'll see about that." She flashed him the peace sign, then stomped off.

The sheriff shuddered, then pointed at me. "I have still got my eye on you. You might be out on bail, but I am going to have you marched to the gallows in no time."

Bruce fixed the sheriff with a steely glare. "Not if I have anything to say about it."

Happy tingles shot through me. Go, Bruce! It was nice having a dashing pirate on my side... though I still had my doubts as to why that was, exactly.

The sheriff's throat bobbed, but he didn't argue with Bruce. Wishing to change the topic from my guilt, I remembered my errand earlier in the evening. "Sheriff, you should look into Bo Erikson." I raised my brows. "He's going around bragging that he killed Macy."

The sheriff scoffed and shared an overly loud laugh with his troll sidekicks. "That twerp? Doesn't have it in him."

I planted a hand on my hip, annoyed at his immediate dismissal of my lead. "You sure? Because his sword was the one sticking out of Macy's chest."

I was pretty sure of it, at least. It *was* a Viking sword, and Bo had been missing his.

My small bluff seemed to pay off. Ol' Sheriff Boswell cleared his throat and pressed his lips together. "We'll look into it."

Bruce winked at me as the sheriff spun on his heel and marched off with his trolls. A few diners nearby threw up rude gestures at his back as he walked away. Good to know I wasn't the only one who wasn't a fan.

I blew out a breath. "That was interesting."

Bruce chuckled. "Interesting takes on a whole new meaning around here." He leaned closer, and my heart fluttered. Was I looking into his dark pools of eyes too long? Oh no, now I was lingering on his lips. Would that thick mustache tickle if we kissed? I shook myself—stop being weird!

"Poppy Lacewing and her crowd of hippie fairies have a somewhat militant attitude toward protecting creatures great and small." Bruce's mustache twitched as he smirked.

Mort looked up from munching on his gyro and blinked his green eyes. "Well she can protect someone else, I thank thee very much." He shook his head and grumbled to himself as he angled for his next bite. "I thought I escaped all such meddling when I abdicated the throne."

I choked. "Sorry—what was that?"

The cat sniffed. "Nothing."

Was that just normal high-and-mighty cat thinking, or was my newly adopted feline actual royalty? That and a thousand other questions would have to wait. For now, I turned back to the pirate across the table from me and tried not to be too flustered by his good looks.

"Think Poppy and her fairy crew would be 'militant' enough to have killed Macy in order to free Mort and the mice?"

Bruce shrugged his broad shoulders. "It's a thought." His gaze grew faraway as he chewed. "If she did kill Macy, why wouldn't Poppy have taken Mort and the mice, then?"

I licked a dribble of tangy tzatziki off my thumb. "Good point. Maybe she thought it would make her look too guilty to take them outright? Or maybe someone approached the tent and she had to run before she had a chance?" Bruce brought up a good point, though. I turned to look at Mort. "Did you see or hear anyone the other night?"

"Besides your snoring?"

My cheeks burned hot. "I do *not* snore."

Bruce politely pretended not to hear.

Mort tipped his head. "I am a heavy sleeper, but I believe I might've heard someone enter the tent at some point. I'm used to Macy coming and going at all hours, though, so I paid it no heed."

I frowned. "If you didn't see or hear anyone, how'd you get out of the cage?"

The tip of Mort's tail flicked side to side, as though he were annoyed at all the questions. "I suppose when Macy died, her spell locking our enclosures died, as well. In any case, when I awoke the lock was sprung and the mice had already absconded."

I shot him a doubtful look as he returned to chowing down on his gyro. Pretty sure if we knew the truth about what happened to those mice, Poppy Lacewing would be giving Mort an earful too.

BROOM CORN

That night I slept more fitfully than I'd expected. I had my own room above the broom shop and a comfortable bed—a big step up from the straw pallet in Macy's tent. Still, I tossed and turned all night with nightmares about creepy *Shining*-esque twins and bloody swords. Eventually, Mort hopped off the foot of the bed, grumbling, and curled up in the window seat.

Thomasina took no mercy on me, though. With only the faintest rays of light peeking through the leaded glass window, she dragged me out of bed to her sunrise yoga class with half a dozen elderly— though spry—women. Witches, actually.

I'd wanted nothing more than to sit back on my haunches in child's pose and go back to sleep, but halfway through Tom's class, I got into a rhythm with the gentle stretches and deep breaths. By the time we rolled up our mats—they must've had a hookup on the outside to get them—I felt refreshed and more like myself than I had in months. It wasn't Pilates—but it was close.

I helped the witch named Julie carry the broom racks back to the middle of the shop floor. We'd pushed everything aside to make room for our class. Apparently, they all took turns hosting and teaching. Julie was a ceramicist and had her own shop selling handmade mugs and plates—yoga was at her place next week.

"I hope you'll lead us through some Pilates next time." Julie shot me a kindly smile. "Once you've been here for a few centuries, you'll understand how exciting trying something new is."

I smiled. "Sure, once I'm settled in. We'll do it soon." My stomach turned a little at the "few centuries" comment. Honestly, I hoped to find a way to break the curse and get back to normal life before I even had a chance to teach.

Also, I felt oddly nervous. I used to think nothing of teaching thirty classes a week. But after I opened my own studio, that had dwindled to only teaching once every few weeks when I covered for an instructor who was out sick. I was badly out of practice.

Julie waggled her gray brows at me as she gathered her bag and mat. "For what it's worth, I think you're one of us."

Helen, a woman with a single white streak through her dark hair, winked. "She means a witch, dear."

Julie held up a finger. "A full witch."

Tom sidled up, her long white hair twisted into twin buns at the base of her neck. I'd been impressed by her headstand—the woman had to be a hundred years old, but she put me to shame at yoga! "The Faire is littered with semi-witches, as we call 'em. People with some kind of specialized power. The cobbler, for instance, can make enchanted shoes, but ask her to cast a spell or divine a prophecy?"

The three women smirked at each other and then burst into laughter. I'd take that as a no-go for the cobbler.

"What makes you think *I* can do that?"

Julie grinned. "The bird, dear, the one you commanded to defecate on your rival's head. There are few magical types that can talk to animals."

My cheeks flushed warm at the term "rival." I'd used some choicer words to describe ol' Meredith.

Tom jerked her chin toward the stairs and Mort, who was still lounging belly up in the windowsill. "Aside from the animals who talk back, of course."

Helen tucked her white streak behind her ear. "You're not a fairy—no wings."

"And if you were a shifter, you'd have more likely turned into a bird and done the deed yourself."

Julie's shoulders shook as she chuckled at her own joke.

Tom clapped a bony hand on my shoulder. "I've got to agree with these gals. We'll get going on your magical training soon." She let out a heavy sigh. "Maybe you'll be better at making enchanted brooms than you are at selling them."

I let out a dry chuckle as we waved goodbye to the other witches and headed upstairs to change. "Well, I can't be any *worse*."

Tom didn't argue with me on that.

Once I'd changed into my purple velvet dress and corset and braided my hair into milkmaid braids like Hilde's, I helped Tom set up a broom display just outside the open door in preparation for the Faire's opening. After we'd gotten squared away and Mort sauntered downstairs (no doubt looking for his next meal) Tom asked me to head over to the Old Renaissance Village.

This was apparently an area dedicated to being somewhat educational. Men and women reenacted what daily life would've been like for peasants during Renaissance times.

"I need you to get me three—no, make it four bundles of broom corn." Tom was already perched on her stool behind the tall counter, deftly sewing bristles together for a new broom.

I raised a brow. "Broom corn?"

She waved me off. "Ask for Gretchen and tell her

I sent you—she'll know what I need. Oh!" She snapped her fingers. "And if you see the carpenter, ask him if he has any polished sticks for me." She lifted a palm. "For the broomstick part."

I nodded. "Naturally."

With some directions from Tom, Mort and I wandered off in search of the peasant village. Though I didn't love the whole "cursed to stay in the Faire for all eternity" thing—and frankly, had probably not even started to come to terms with it —I had to admit that the Faire was actually pretty fun. Visitors started to pour in the gates wearing everything from jeans to highly elaborate costumes.

The delicious scents of roasted turkey and sweet pastries filled the air, along with the peaceful strumming of harps and jaunty singing of sea shanties. I had a new appreciation for the Faire, now that I knew the fairies were real fairies and the mermaids weren't just holding their breath underwater.

Soon, Mort and I found the peasant village. Unlike the rest of the brightly colored, highly whimsical shops and costumes, the peasant village was drab. Sour-faced women in brown dresses and bonnets worked at spinning wheels, while stony-faced men in mud-covered knickers tilled a small garden.

Yikes—had somebody died? My stomach clenched. Aside from Macy Mulligan, of course.

Now which one of these *super cheery* peasants was Gretchen?

Mort made a noise like he was hacking up a hairball. I glanced down at where he stood beside my ankles. "Peasants." He shuddered. "Always filthy and ungrateful and threatening an uprising over every little thing."

I opened my mouth to ask him if this was another reference to his stint as a king, but was interrupted by a loud, jarring voice.

"'Allo, there! You need sumptin'?"

I warily approached the woman who sat in the dirt, listlessly hacking at the soil with a small hoe.

"I'm looking for Gretchen? I'm supposed to purchase some broom corn for—"

The woman sucked in a breath, and her pale eyes lit up. "You're that new witch, the one who killed Macy Mulligan!" She looked round at her fellow, less enthusiastic peasants. "Hey! It's the woman 'at killed Macy Mulligan!"

A few peasants cast bleak looks our way, then immediately returned to their manual labor.

She made a show of taking off her imaginary cap and bowing to me. "I'm Lavinia."

"Laidey. But I didn't actually kill anyone." And why did that name sound familiar?

Lavinia gave me an exaggerated wink that required the use of most of her facial muscles. "Sure you didn't."

Suddenly, the name clicked. Hilde had told me about her. "You're Macy's former—er…" Was indentured servant a slur?

"Slave, yes." Lavinia, her hair covered with a dirt-colored scarf, nodded. "Recently earned my freedom, but oh, that I had your stones to off her meself!" She clasped her hands together at her chest and gazed longingly at the bright summer sky. "Oh, that I'd been a fly on the wall."

For the murder?! This lady was off her rocker. I shot Mort a wide-eyed look. He raised his little cat brows and muttered, "Peasants. They art all crazy."

Though it begged the question. If Lavinia hated Macy so much…

I leaned into one hip. "By the by… why *didn't* you kill her yourself?"

Lavinia pressed her hands to her heart, her nails caked in mud. "Not for lack of trying, mum." She shook her head. "Macy was a powerful witch—it's why it took another one like you to kill her."

I frowned. Here was another person telling me I was a powerful witch when all I'd done was get a falcon to poop.

Lavinia curled her lip, revealing a few missing teeth. "She always put protection spells up around her tent at night *and* her portion of it. Tried a few times to get her in the night—never worked."

I frowned. If that was true, how did the killer get around Macy's protection spells? Were they just that powerful? Or had the killer been someone Macy knew and trusted enough to let in?

Lavinia chuckled. "Even tried drugging her, you know, so she'd pass out before she had a chance to cast her defensive spells. But she only took her meals from the vendors themselves. Wouldn't let me anywhere near her food and drink. Probably a smart move…"

I curled my lip. Definitely. I couldn't believe this woman was openly admitting to trying to murder Macy. Then again, if she was the killer, it seemed unlikely that she'd be bragging to me about it, versus trying to hide it. Plus, why kill Macy after finally earning her freedom?

Lavinia pointed me to Gretchen—honestly, they almost looked identical—who got about gathering broom corn for me. It was apparently a plant that looked just like corn, except without the actual corn cob. While I waited on Tom's order, I thought over the peasant's words.

Maybe the killer was someone Macy let into the tent. Then again, she'd been out at the pub—could someone there have slipped some sort of potion into her drink, like Lavinia had tried to? If they had, Macy would've fallen asleep before casting her protective spells over the tent, allowing the killer to sneak in.

I shuddered. Either way, there was a murderer

running around the Faire, and it was becoming clearer than ever that Macy had plenty of enemies.

Finding the real killer and clearing my name was not going to be easy. And I only had three days until my trial to do it.

CAT AND MOUSE

*B*y the time I got back to Swept Away with the broom corn (why did this still sound like a made-up thing?), Thomasina was happily assisting some non-magical visitors. Not wanting to interrupt, I deposited the raw material outside the back door. As I came around to the front again, an act onstage caught my eye.

Swept Away had a prime location at the intersection of a couple of main thoroughfares. A big open space in the middle formed a sort of town square with a stone fountain and a stage kitty-corner to the shop. A tall, elegant-looking man—or probably elf, judging by the pointed ears—stood with one hand pressed to his heart, a small skull in the other. I really hoped that wasn't real.

"To be, or not to be. That is the question."

"The *question* is, when is this lousy show over?"

The large crowd laughed at the heckler's joke, while the elf's face flushed bright red. He pushed on, doing his best to ignore the chant that started up.

"Whether 'tis nobler of the mind—"

"Cat and Mouse! Cat and Mouse!"

I frowned. That'd been Macy's show. Right on cue, Mort lifted his chin. "My adoring public awaits."

I chuckled, then recalled something Macy had said about having the most popular showtimes. "Is this when your show would normally have gone on?"

Mort shrugged. "I'm a cat. I do not tell time."

I waited.

"Fine. Yes, this seems about the time. We would perform again in the afternoon."

"Interesting." The act that had replaced Macy's didn't seem nearly as popular. I wanted to get a closer look. Mort and I padded across the square together, dodging the man showing off his hacky sack skills. Mort and I hung back at the edge of the angry crowd that was quickly turning into a mob.

"—by a sleep, to say we end—Oh shut up!" The elf finally lost his cool. He whirled to face the jeering crowd, his face nearly purple and his long arms stiff at his sides.

"Thou art boils! Thou art sodden-faced fools! Ai!" The Shakespeare-spouting elf cringed back as a turkey leg whizzed past his face.

"Boo!" Men and women cupped their hands to their mouths and shouted at the frazzled elf.

"By my troth!" Mort's green eyes widened. "Methinks they mean to tear that elf limb from limb. They miss me. By truth, they doth really miss me."

I shot him a look and mumbled out of the corner of my mouth so no one would see me talking to a cat, "And they miss Macy and the mice, right?"

Mort sat and waved a paw. "Right, sure."

The elf shrieked as a tankard barely missed his feathered cap and spilled beer all over the raised wooden stage. He pointed a trembling finger at the offender. "A pox upon you!" He turned his furious gaze to address the whole rowdy crowd. "A pox upon all of you foppish louts! Why, you're nothing but a gaggle of scullions and churles, you filthy—"

"Alright, alright. We put on a clean show here." A well-dressed man with huge, velvet damask sleeves and a white ruff around his neck hurried the cursing elf offstage. He waved a ring-covered hand at the unruly crowd and shouted to be heard above all the ruckus.

"We would all love to see the world famous Cat and Mouse show."

The crowd cheered and pumped their fists in the air. Huh. Maybe Macy hadn't been exaggerating her popularity. I glanced down at Mort, who primly lifted his chin and gave me a smug blink.

The guy in the fancy clothes winced. "But alas!

'Tis terrible news, but unfortunately Macy Mulligan has left our sweet Faire forever."

"What?"

"Where's she gone?"

"What happened?"

The man ignored all the shouted questions and sprinted offstage behind a curtain. Gradually the grumbling crowd dispersed to wreak drunken havoc elsewhere, and Mort and I threaded forward.

"Where art we going?"

I lifted my chin to keep an eye on my target—the curtain that led backstage. "To be nosy." I couldn't really say for sure that this had anything to do with Macy's death, but this was her show's time slot, and the crowd had been cheering for her. Maybe I could pick up some tidbits that might give me some new leads.

Mort and I slipped through the red curtain into a tight alleyway between the stage and the next building over. We crept forward until we reached the corner that led to the open area directly behind the stage.

"I gaveth you a fair chance, Eldor. Thou hast been pushing for this opportunity for years now." The well-dressed man shook his head, which sent the feather in his cap bobbing. "The crowd hath spoken." He flashed his eyes at the fuming elf, Eldor, who paced in front of him, kicking up dust with his curly-toed boots.

"They proved, just now, why Macy had that time slot and not you." He softened his tone. "I'm sorry."

"Fie!" Eldor whirled to face the man who'd ushered him offstage. "'Tis a travesty! 'Tis an—an outrage!" He scoffed. "Those bumpkins wouldn't know culture if it slapped them in the face!"

That was quite the image.

The other man shrugged. "My apologies, Eldor, thou knoweth I am but a mouthpiece for the king." He sighed. "Listen, I shall giveth you through the end of the week, but thou hast got to turn this around. If you don't, we shall have to puteth you back at your old time slot."

Eldor grumbled something and marched off. The other man let out a heavy sigh and called after him, "Anon!"

He got no reply.

I took that opportunity to walk around the corner and get some answers. I feared that argument might in fact be related to Macy's death.

"Oh!" The balding man pressed a hand to his chest. "Oh. Thou hast startled me."

I gave him a sheepish look. "Sorry. I'm Laidey." I gestured to the cat at my side. "And this is Mort."

The man sucked in a breath and crouched down in front of my black cat. "*The* Mort?"

"As I live and breathe," my cat drawled.

The man pressed a hand to his chest. "I am Councilor Highbury. So pleased to maketh your acquaintance. I mostly dealt with Macy whilst she was alive, but you were our most popular show." His eyes widened. "Any chance you mighteth get the ol' act back together again?"

Mort shook his head. "Apologies, good sir, but I fear we hath lost the mice as well as Macy."

"Lost, or ate?" I muttered.

Mort glared at me, then turned back to Councilor Highbury.

"Wouldst thou consider a solo act?"

Mort sniffed, his tiny black nose in the air. "I am flattered, sir, truly. But my time upon the stage is over. 'Tis time I retired."

"Ah, I was afeared you might say that." The councilor patted his thigh, then rose with a grunt. "But I understand. Best to go out on a high note."

Mort nodded.

What had this act been that made him and the mice so popular? I'd have to get the scoop from my cat later. I stopped the councilor before he wandered off.

"Uh—actually, I was just curious." I tried for an innocent smile. "Since I'm new here… you're the one in charge of programming the acts?"

Highbury narrowed his dark eyes. "Why doth thou ask? Dost thou covet Macy Mulligan's time slot as well?"

I waved my hands and shook my head. "No. No! No, absolutely not." If the idea of getting onstage had terrified me before, the thought now, after witnessing that angry mob moments ago, had me breaking into a cold sweat.

Highbury softened. "Good. Apologies. I just get my fair share of hangers-on, you know, always begging favors." He rolled his eyes.

"Like Eldor?"

He nodded. "Eldor Glenhaven's a good chap. Refined, knows his Shakespeare." He huffed. "But that's not what the crowd wants. They want to be *entertained*, not educated." He stepped closer and brought one hand to the side of his mouth, as though letting me in on a secret. "Truth be told, I'm the one who decides which act goes on when. I haveth the king's ear, aye, but I'd never harass him with such petty goings-on." He smirked. "But 'tis handy to blame the allotments on the king when the 'talent' gets upset."

I nodded. "And Eldor was upset because you wouldn't give him Macy's time slot?"

Councilor Highbury rolled his eyes. "I finally relented and let him have his shot, but you saw what happened up there. 'Twas nearly a bloodbath. He's been lobbying me, day in and out, for Macy's spot for years. He thought such a lowbrow act, his words —" He shot an apologetic look at Mort.

"No offense, good sir."

"Well, he didn't think it deserved the prime spots." The councilor splayed his gloved hands. "But

Macy and her cat and mice—they put on a good show. And the audience loved it!" He looked once more at Mort. "Thou art sure I cannot convince you to make go of it?" He raised his brows. "I could have someone look into breaking that curse on you? The king hath deep pockets."

Mort swiped a paw. "'Tis a generous offer, but my mind has been made."

The councilor nodded his acquiescence and shuffled off, while Mort and I headed back toward the broom shop. I shot him a curious look.

"What made your show so popular? I had no idea what a star you were."

He offered me a flat look, then lifted his nose and tail. "I'll have you know that the mice and I performed death-defying feats of agility."

I shot the overweight cat a dubious look. I mean, I wasn't one to judge—I was out of shape myself. But you didn't hear me bragging about my agility, either.

"Like what?"

Mort sniffed as we slipped past the cart where you could have a candle molded into the shape of your hand.

"I'd walk the tightrope, leap through rings of fire, perform acrobatics like balancing atop Macy's head while she juggled knives." He shrugged. "And the mice would balance atop mine."

I curled my lip. "Sounds dangerous."

"'Twas. And demeaning. But it was honest."

I frowned. "And what did the councilor mean about breaking your curse?"

He scoffed as we reached the entrance to the now empty broom shop and stood in the shade of the doorway. "Ha! Didst thou think I was a talking cat?" He lifted his face and shouted at Tom, who sat behind the counter. "She thought I was a talking cat!"

My new boss threw her head back and cackled.

I rolled my eyes. "How foolish of me." Right. Because in a place where curses, witches, elves, and fairies were real, the idea of a talking cat was just laughable.

Mort shook his head as we walked inside. "No. Long, long ago, I once was a man."

I frowned. "I'm not sure I want you sleeping in my room anymore."

He rolled his eyes. "Groweth up. I've been a cat about a thousand years longer than I was a man."

I stopped in my tracks. Was that just hyperbole? I shuddered as I considered how long "forever" might mean if I didn't find a way to escape the Faire's curse. First things first, though. I needed to keep the sheriff from lopping my head off by solving the mystery of who'd really killed Macy Mulligan.

And that uppity, Shakespeare-spouting elf, Eldor, had just made my list of suspects.

TURKEY LEGS

After a frustrating day of Thomasina training me in the art of broom making, the Faire closed its gates—with me still trapped inside. I bolted the shutters over the big front window as Tom counted the money at the counter. A thought had been bugging me.

"What about my friends and family? Won't they notice I'm not answering my phone and send the police to find me?"

Tom didn't bother glancing up. "Twenty-eight—twenty-nine... Nah. I'm not sure why, but I suppose it's part of the curse. I think our friends and family just sort of forget about us."

I cringed. "That's sad."

"C'est la vie." Mort weaved between racks of handcrafted brooms, his tail in the air. "I feel great hunger. Prithee, let us get some dinner."

I looked to Tom, who waved me off. "Knock yourselves out." She tossed me a gold coin, and I was proud of my coordination when I caught it.

"Care to join us?"

She glanced up, surprised. "Er... thanks." The hint of a smile tugged at the corner of her mouth. "Not tonight. I've got plans with the gals."

"The coven?"

She nodded. "Maybe next time." I headed toward the door. "Oh, and Adelaide?" I turned around, and Tom winked. "It gets easier."

"I sure hope so," I grumbled as Mort and I dipped out into the dusky village street. "Let's go find Hilde —maybe she has some time off for dinner."

As we bent our steps toward the food court, I rolled my shoulders and cracked my neck. Broom making, or squiring as Tom put it, was no joke. I'd spent countless ten-hour days in Pilates teacher training, my mind and body aching by the end of a long weekend. I knew from experience that learning a worthwhile craft took patience, hard work, and enduring a steep learning curve.

But broom making? Come on! It was a stick and some smaller bushier sticks—how hard could it be?

Super hard, apparently.

Tom had explained that the broomsticks had to be made from certain trees to impart certain powers, dried for sometimes over a year, polished but not varnished, the weight and balance carefully tested—

ERIN JOHNSON

especially for flying brooms—and the length adjusted for different heights.

And that was just the stick part! The bristles—their various materials, plaiting, lengths, density, and sewing methods—were a whole other story. Add to that learning to use some ancient machine called a kick winder and then bespelling said brooms, and my head was spinning.

Luckily, the line at the Pull My Turkey Leg booth wasn't too long yet, and Mort and I soon edged up to the order counter.

Hilde, her cheeks flushed and hairline damp from what had no doubt been a long day, still flashed me a bright smile. She dipped her head and curtsied. "M'lady! I'm so pleased you've come to visit."

I was too tired to remind her I wasn't actually a lady and tried to ignore the snickers in line behind me. "Hi, Hilde! Still working your shift, huh?"

She nodded, her blonde locks once again wrapped over the top of her head in milkmaid braids. "Have to keep at it until the whole Faire 'as been served."

She worked so hard. I badly wanted Hilde to find her stride and bust her way out of the turkey booth.

"Keep it movin'!" a man in a stained apron shouted from the blisteringly hot grill behind her.

She shot me an apologetic smile. "What'll you have?"

I ordered turkey legs for Mort and me (what

else?) and a tankard of grog, aka beer. I needed it after the day I'd had.

Mort lifted a paw. "Make it two."

I blinked down at where he sat next to me. "Can cats have beer?"

"That is for me to know, and thou to findest out."

I begrudgingly flashed two fingers at Hilde. I wasn't sure I wanted to "findest" out if it meant cleaning up cat puke later. Mort's hairballs were already more than enough, thank you.

I passed Hilde my gold coin as she slid two foaming tankards over the counter to me. "Any chance you can take a break and join us?"

Her shoulders slumped, and she let out a heavy sigh. "'Fraid not, m'lady." Her blue eyes darted behind me, and I turned to see the line of Rennies stretching dozens deep. In fact, long lines stood in front of all the food places... except for the empty bread bowl place. Nothing but crickets there... and those two creepy twin kids again.

Hilde swept a hand across her flushed, damp brow. It must be miserable working all day in that heat. We had to figure out what kind of magic Hilde had, and what she'd excel at. Then again, I still wasn't convinced I knew what my own magic was. Were the yoga biddies right and I was a witch like them?

"Oh!" Hilde brightened. "Tomorrow's my day off

—first one in weeks." She beamed. "Maybe we could get together then?"

I grinned as I scooped up our paper plates of turkey legs, tucking the tankards under my arms. A balancing spell would be helpful right about now. "Sounds great!"

She greeted the next customer as we headed off. "Welcome to Pull My Turkey Leg, what'll you 'ave?"

Mort and I found a picnic table—they were quickly filling up. I took a deep drink of my ice-cold beer and sighed happily. As I lowered the tankard, I was startled to find Bruce standing in front of me, grinning.

"That looks good."

I chuckled. "I needed this after the day I had."

He winked. "The beer, too."

Mort took a break from lapping at his own beer to groan.

The pirate captain chuckled and gestured at the bench across from me. "May I?"

As he settled in, I found myself babbling all about my day, the mind-boggling process of broom making, and eventually my suspicions about Macy's former servant, Lavinia, and the jealous elf, Eldor.

Bruce leaned forward, his crossed arms resting on the table, and nodded. "Sounds like you've had a busy day."

I sniffed my agreement and took another swig of beer. "Sorry, I've been blathering."

"Hear, hear," Mort muttered as he chomped at his turkey leg.

But the pirate's thick 'stache twitched. "I like listening to you talk."

My cheeks flushed hot, and I suddenly found my nearly empty plate fascinating. "How was your day?"

"Ah, well." Bruce waved a gloved hand. "Swash-bucklingly dull compared to yours. Had a crew meeting, studied my poetry, and spoke to my accountant about some treasure investments."

I chuckled and looked up at him—if he was joking, I couldn't tell. "Poetry? Really?"

He shot me a challenging look, though his dark eyes held a twinkle. "Despite the rumors, pirates *can* read, you know."

I smiled. "I didn't mean that. It's just... it seems a pretty urbane hobby for a pirate captain."

He reached across the table and took a piece of turkey leg from my plate. He looked off thoughtfully as he chewed.

I wasn't sure why it made me happy that he'd eaten off my plate, but it did.

"I dearly miss sailing the high seas. Nothing compares to the wind in your sails and naught but an endless, churning expanse all around."

I leaned my cheek into my hand. I could believe the poetry now. I could practically feel the sea spray from the way he spoke about the ocean.

Bruce sighed and shot me a playful look. "But I

find I do not miss the pillaging and plundering. Nasty business. These days, I am full content to study my poems and spend half the day gazing up at the clouds in the sky." His tone shifted as he studied my face. "Stargazing isn't half bad, either, if one has the right companion."

I gulped and looked down. The way my cheeks were burning, they had to be bright pink.

"Get thou a room," Mort muttered from his spot on the bench beside me.

Bruce patted the table and turned casual again. "You'll be surprised the hobbies you take up after you've been here awhile." He winked at me. "Maybe I'll take up broom squiring."

I grinned back. "And maybe I'll take up poetry."

He pressed a gloved hand to his breast and looked up and away.

"FULL FATHOM five thy father lies;
    Of his bones are coral made;
    Those are pearls that were his eyes:
    Nothing of him that doth fade,
    But doth suffer a sea-change
    Into something rich and strange."

SMILING, I shook my head.
    "Shakespeare."

"Ah. It's lovely." I chuckled. "Though based on the reaction to Eldor's performance earlier, I wouldn't recommend taking your poetry to the stage."

"Duly noted."

I looked up, frowning as I thought of Eldor. Even if the elf was the killer, it didn't explain how he'd managed to get past Macy Mulligan's protection spell. I thought over what Lavinia had told me about her attempted murders.

"Would a spell or potion show up in an autopsy report?"

Bruce's dark eyes widened. "Planning to do me in already? I'll keep my poetry to myself from now on."

I smirked. "No." I leaned closer and lowered my voice. Though the hubbub of the tables around us filled the night air with boisterous laughter and lively conversation, I didn't want anyone to know I was looking into Macy's case. "I meant, would it have shown up in Macy's system? Her former servant suggested someone might have drugged her so that she'd fall asleep before casting her nightly protection spells."

Bruce nodded, thoughtful. "Thereby allowing the killer entry." He shrugged. "Well, there is one way to find out. After you finish eating, I'll take you to the torture dungeon."

I spluttered and nearly choked on some turkey leg. Bruce jumped to his feet, alarmed and no doubt

ready to Heimlich me—did pirates know first aid?—
but I waved him off.

"Apologies, that sounded far worse than I meant
it to."

I nodded. "It's okay."

Bruce smiled. "It's just that that's where our in-
Faire coroner-slash-vampire works."

I gawked at him. Was that supposed to make me
feel *better*?

THE DUNGEON OF DESPAIR

"The Dungeon of Despair?" I looked from the sign above the chained, spiked doors to Bruce. "Seriously?"

The pirate shrugged.

"Can't we at least come back during the day?" I rubbed my goose-pimpled arms. The moon hovered high in the sky, eerie clouds drifting across it.

Bruce shot me an apologetic look. "Vampires don't really do the daytime."

I whimpered.

"Oh, don't be a turkey leg." Mort, tail in the air, trotted around the side of the building and led the way through a couple of gates to the back door.

Bruce knocked, then leaned close. Close enough for me to smell the rich leather of the straps crossing his chest.... My gaze drifted to his lips. Hoo boy. I shook myself. It'd been way too long since a man got that close to me. I needed to get ahold of myself.

"Don't worry." Bruce gave me a steady, encouraging smile. "Vern gave up drinking from live people centuries ago."

I gave a weak chuckle. "Oh, phew. So relieved." I'd gone from being an out-of-work Pilates teacher to meeting real live (er, undead?) vampires.

What was my life?

Locks clicked and slid, and the heavy wooden door creaked open, revealing a sliver of darkness beyond.

"Enter, little suns," a silvery voice drawled.

This was not filling me with confidence.

"Ladies first."

I shot Bruce an incredulous look, but he flashed his charming smile and chuckled. "Just joking."

I scoffed, torn between giggling and stomping my foot. "You'd better be."

He laughed harder. We climbed down a dim stairwell, then stepped into a cavernous museum of torture instruments. These must be the vampire's private pieces, stored below the public museum up above.

It was pretty much what I'd expected. Magically sparkling overhead spotlights cut through the thick darkness and starkly illuminated gruesome displays of mannequins on the rack and in that spikey sarcophagus thing. Sharp knives and spiked clubs glinted on the walls.

And, to my utter horror, in the center of it all, a body lay under a sheet on a slab. I gulped. Pretty sure that one wasn't a mannequin. A lock of Macy's curly orange hair peeked out from underneath. Yep, definitely not a mannequin.

"Vern?" Bruce looked about.

"Yes, fair ones."

I shrieked as a tall, pale man appeared in front of us—literally *appeared* out of nowhere!

Mort arched his back and hissed. "Gads, man!"

I glanced at Bruce, my heart pounding against my chest. "Vern?"

The pirate captain, who looked as shaken as I felt, nodded.

Vern slid in front of me, his dark eyes large and eager, as though he were drinking me in. "I don't believe I've had the pleasure." The hint of a sharp fang peeked from between his full lips.

I managed a weak smile. "I'm Adelaide—Laidey."

He shook a dark, wavy lock out of his eyes. "Dr. Vernadsky Kostyuk."

He emphasized the "doctor" part.

"But you may call me Vern, dear one."

Dear one, eh? Laying it on a little thick, weren't we, Dr. Vern? I cleared my throat and tried to ignore the intense and supremely creepy way he was looking at me.

"Doctor, hm? So do you also practice medicine or just..." I swept a hand at the body on the slab and finished the sentence in my head—*or just cut up corpses and collect torture devices.*

"Oh no." Vern swept over to the metal autopsy table, his movements fluid and careful. "Medical school in the Middle Ages mostly consisted of Leeches 101 and Bloodletting." He pressed his lips together. "I suppose I actually haven't strayed too far from that last one." His tinkling laughter sent shivers down my spine.

I sent Bruce a slightly nauseated look. "Oh. That was humor."

He flashed his eyes back.

"But I do my best to keep up with the latest science."

"Great." I was ready to get out of el creepo's torture chamber/morgue. I cleared my throat and tipped my head toward the dead body on the table next to a tray of sharp, pointy instruments. "We actually came by to ask you a couple of questions about Macy Mulligan."

"Oh?" Vern arched a sculpted brow as he hovered over her body.

I nodded. "Have you performed her autopsy yet?"

Vern pressed his hands to his cold, dead heart and grimaced. "Oh, little bunny, I did. You just missed it, in fact. My apologies."

It took me a moment to catch on. I did my best to

hide my disgust. "Oh, no. No no no." I waved my hands. "I didn't want to watch. I just wanted to know if you'd determined the cause of death?"

The vampire nodded, deadly serious. "It was the enormous Viking sword through her chest."

Facepalm. Bruce looked like he was trying not to smirk.

Mort, who sat at my feet, shook his little cat head. "Groundbreaking stuff, this."

"Sorry, I meant... did you find anything else in her system? That might have contributed to her death?" I lifted a palm. "Specifically, do you know if she had a spell on her or—"

"Fairy dust." Vern swept a long hand at Macy's covered body. "I discovered a significant quantity in her stomach." He tipped his head, thoughtfully. "Also, ale, meat casings, and rodent hair."

I could've done without that last tidbit.

"Even I find that revolting," my cat drawled.

"You're sure? Fairy dust?"

The vampire nodded at Bruce.

The pirate turned to me and raised his brows. "That lends some credence to your theory that Macy was drugged."

"Oh, undoubtedly." Vern rubbed his pale hands together at his chest, like he was plotting something. "She'd have slept like a baby." He smiled gently at the corpse. "Wouldn't have felt a thing."

I couldn't control my shudder. "Well, great meeting you, Vern. Thanks for your help."

Bruce, Mort, and I hustled through the dimly lit dungeon toward the stairs up to the side door.

"Do come again soon…" His eerie voice trailed out after us into the night.

I certainly hoped to "come again" never.

FAIRY DUST

idmorning the next day, Hilde swung by the broom shop on her day off. I asked Thomasina if I could take a break to walk the Faire with her.

"Go!" Tom waved me off while she deftly bundled bunches of dried broom corn together.

She was clearly devastated to lose the world's worst broom saleswoman for half an hour.

Mort, Hilde, and I strolled down the crowded village lanes, weaving between families and tourists, and browsing the various shops and carts. I filled my new friend in on what we'd discovered at the Dungeon of Despair/morgue last night.

"Vern told us that Macy had fairy powder in her stomach. So much that it was clear she'd been drugged."

Hilde grimaced and wrung her dainty hands together. "You went to see Dr. Vern, m'lady?"

I'd given up trying to correct her that it was just Laidey.

She shuddered. "I admire yer bravery, I do. That place gives me the frights."

I nodded. "Oh believe me, I was freaked out. I'd never have been able to go if it weren't for Bruce going along, too."

Mort huffed. "I thinkest thou art forgetting someone."

"Really?"

I carried the chonk of a cat in my arms like a baby, his head lolling to the side. Within minutes of leaving Swept Away, he'd complained of being too tired to walk. Apparently, his morning of lounging in the sunbeams on the windowsill had been too rigorous, and he needed to be carried.

"Bruce escorted you?" Hilde shot me a sly smile. "Methinks the pirate captain might have feelings for you, m'lady."

My cheeks flushed hot, and I looked down at my feet. My red-sneaker-covered feet. Eventually, I'd probably have to update my footwear to some Renaissance-appropriate boots that didn't clash with my long skirts and corset. But for now, I enjoyed the tie to my normal life. They made me feel like I was still myself.

"Ah. He's very charming, but he probably flirts

with all the new girls who get cursed." After Chad's betrayal, I found I had a new, and probably self-destructive, distrust of any good-looking man who showed an interest in me. I interpreted it as the first step on a journey that would ultimately lead to betrayal and heartbreak.

Super healthy outlook.

One I should probably work on. But my trial was the day after tomorrow, and I had my hands full trying not to get drawn and quartered by the sheriff, and then figuring out a way to break the curse. Working through my emotional issues would have to wait.

Hilde shrugged. "Well, I don't know much about him." She lifted her blond brows. "I could ask around for ya, m'lady?"

I grinned, torn. On one hand it felt a bit "high school" to get the scoop on Bruce through the rumor mill. On the other hand, I was still trying to find my place in the Faire—not that I planned on staying if I could help it. Any information about the relationships and dynamics of the place would probably help me get my bearings.

I bit my lip. "Thanks for the offer, Hilde. I'll think about it. In the meantime, do you know where the fairies hang out? I want to ask someone about that fairy powder."

"Well, the queen and her lot lounge all day in the Enchanted Forest. But if yer lookin' for a fairy who'll sell you powder…" Hilde tugged me down a narrow alleyway, shaded and cool. The day was cranking up to be a scorcher—and humid too.

I glanced down at the fat (and increasingly heavy) cat in my arms. I hoped we wouldn't run into that Poppy Lacewing fairy. I might be tempted to hand Mort over to her.

"Oops—gnomes. Best we pick up our pace."

Little bearded, red-capped gnomes—looking exactly like their plastic lawn ornament counterparts —burrowed up from the ground.

"Heh!"

They leered at me from the shadows behind crates and chomped their teeth.

I curled my lip and ran after my friend. We didn't slow until we reached the bright sunshine at the other end.

"The gnomes—" Hilde's chest heaved as she caught her breath. "The infestation follows us everywhere the Faire goes. Be mindful anytime ya duck down an alley."

Mort, still heavy in my arms, nodded his agreement. "Their bites do stingeth something fierce."

I glanced behind us, where dozens of beady eyes watched us, glinting in the shadows at the mouth to the alley. I shuddered—I definitely did not want to add gnome bites to my list of problems.

As Hilde led us to the outskirts of the Faire, and then through the gates that led to the Rennie field of tents, caravans, and camps, my heart sped up with unease. I had flashbacks to Macy basically kidnapping me… and waking up next to her corpse in the tent.

I shuddered, and Mort groaned. "Stop your fidgeting, you disrupt my rest."

"Oh, brother." I rolled my eyes and deposited the cat on the grassy ground. My arms had been burning since we passed the pickle cart.

Mort grumbled to himself, "Backeth when I was king, I'd never have tolerated such treatment."

I snorted. "King? Of what, the other alley cats?"

He hissed at me just as Poppy Lacewing and her colorful band of fairies looked up.

Perfect.

They lounged in the shade of some nearby trees. While Poppy looked like a perfectly boho fairy with her plaited blond locks and giant flower crown, ready for some Instagram shots at an indie music festival, others of her gang looked like they'd never left Woodstock. One fairy slowly fluttered her tie-dyed wings, while another swayed and snapped her fingers, grooving to some nonexistent tunes. And was that pink-haired one literally hugging the tree?

As soon as Poppy registered Mort—and the fact that he'd just hissed at me—she leapt to her tiny, bare feet and stomped over to us. A few of her fellow hippies drifted after her.

"Peace." She flashed me two fingers, then scowled

at Hilde, Mort, and me. "Are you here to hand over the cat?"

"The cat hath a name," Mort grumbled, his tail swishing from side to side with agitation.

"Whoa, man, kind of a harsh vibe over here." A fairy in a white cotton muumuu placed a gentle hand on Poppy's shoulder.

Another sprite with round, pink-lensed glasses floated over and laid her head on Poppy's shoulder. "Yeah, what's the bummer?"

Poppy pursed her lips. "This is the witch who offed Macy Mulligan and won't give me her cat *or* mice." She flipped one long blond braid over her tanned shoulder.

"Ooh, heavy."

"What's the hangup?" The one in glasses blinked at me.

I rolled my eyes. "To be honest, I have no idea where the mice are."

Poppy gasped.

I threw my hand down at Mort. "And the cat can obviously speak for himself."

"Thank thee, hippie fairies, but I would rather that one"—he jerked his little chin at Poppy—"does not bogart me, in your parlance. I am quite comfortable with my current arrangement."

I'd carried him like a baby all around the Faire. He'd *better* be comfortable with it.

Poppy crossed her arms and huffed. "Then why are you here?"

The muumuu fairy blinked her bloodshot eyes at Poppy. "Get off of it, man."

"Yeah. Don't be a downer."

Poppy huffed and stomped off toward the shady tree—and the fairy wrapped around it.

Muumuu shrugged. "Sorry, man. She's been kinda off lately. Ya dig?"

Off? "Why?"

Rose-colored glasses shook her head and fluttered her gossamer wings. "No idea. Maybe she's fried."

Hilde leaned close and brought her hand to the side of her mouth. "Sometimes these fairies do partake of their own supply."

Got it. Which reminded me...

"I actually wanted to ask if you'd sold any fairy dust lately?"

Muumuu's bloodshot eyes widened. "No way!"

"Why? You the fuzz or something?" The other fairy shot me a dubious look. "If you're a cop, you have to tell us."

I scoffed. "Hardly. The *fuzz* threw me in the pillory the other day and wants to see my head roll."

Muumuu squinted her glassy eyes at me. "Oh, yeah. I remember you. I saw a kid throw an old tomato at your head. Bummer."

I nodded. "Yeah. Super bummer. About that fairy dust, though?" These two seemed so fried I wasn't sure I'd get anything out of them. I hated to say it, but I almost wished Poppy would come back. She might be angry and militant, but at least she was lucid.

Muumuu shook her head at me. "We do not sell fairy dust. That is not legal in the Faire, and we are law-abiding fairies."

The one in the round glasses flitted closer and lowered her voice to a stage whisper. "Under the table though, sure. How much do you need?"

Uh. I glanced at Hilde, who shrugged. I hadn't been planning on actually purchasing any—I just wanted to know if they'd sold some to anyone who might want Macy dead. But maybe it wouldn't hurt to buy a little—I *had* been having trouble sleeping lately.

I nodded, though I had no idea the units one bought fairy dust in. An ounce? A brick? A thimble? "How about enough to really knock me out cold for the night. I want to sleep like a baby."

Muumuu nodded, knowingly. "Right on."

Glasses held out her palm. "That'll be ten gold coins."

"Fie!" Mort yowled. "What art thou? Racketeers?"

I gaped. I didn't have the best grasp of the Faire's currency, but if a day's work earned me a single gold coin, then a week and a half's worth of wages for one dose seemed exorbitant.

Muumuu shrugged and fluttered her wings. "I know it's a lot of bread, man, but fairy dust is pretty rare stuff."

The one in glasses nodded. "Pretty trippy though." She held out her palm. "You dig?"

I scoffed. "No. I do not dig." I shook my head. "I can't afford that."

Muumuu shrugged. "Plenty of people are willing to pay for it, man."

"Like who, exactly?" I needed some names.

The other fairy narrowed her eyes behind her tinted glasses. "I dunno. You ask a lot of questions for someone who isn't the fuzz." She jerked her head at her friend in the muumuu. "Peace!"

They flashed me the peace sign and flitted back into the shade with the other dozen or so fairies.

Hilde whimpered. "Apologies that weren't a more fruitful trip, m'lady."

"It's okay." Mort, Hilde, and I wandered back to the Faire. "We may not have gotten any names, but now that I know how expensive it is, it narrows down our list of suspects."

"My bet is on that Poppy Lacewing."

I nodded down at my cat. "She's definitely a top suspect. Poppy had the easiest access to the fairy dust. And Vern said he'd found quite a lot in Macy's stomach. You either need to have the money to buy the dust, or to be a fairy and have it at your little sparkly fingertips."

Hilde shook her head. "It probably wasn't poor Lavinia then. She were just barely able to buy her freedom."

I nodded. "Good point. She's probably out." I quirked my lips to the side as we passed through the gates and back into the bustling Faire. Looked like it'd gotten even busier in the short time we'd left.

"Eldor, the elf, was well-dressed and seemed fancy. He might have had the money."

"What about that Viking lad? Bo Erikson?" Mort hugged close to my ankles as we skirted around the sword swallower.

I nodded. "It was his sword used to kill Macy, and he bragged about doing it. But he didn't seem to actually have been in her tent that night. Not sure his financial situation, though—it's worth looking into."

Hilde clicked her tongue. "It's probably not Kip then, either."

I frowned, puzzled. "Who?"

Hilde's blue eyes widened. "Didn't I mention Kip? He's Macy's ex-husband. But I don't think he or Nell —that's his new wife—could've afforded the fairy dust. Not with all the rumors of people finding hair and rodent droppings in their soup."

I sucked in a breath. "Wait!" I'd met Nell when I ordered a bread bowl from their restaurant the other night—before Bruce intervened and saved me from food poisoning. "So Macy's ex is the bread bowl guy, huh?"

Hilde nodded. "Macy and Kip fought like cats and dogs—beg your pardon," she added to Mort.

He graciously nodded his head. "No offense taken."

Huh. I'd need to look into Kip and his contaminated bread bowls. Right after finishing my shift at the broom shop.

INHERITANCE

*H*ilde accompanied me and Mort back to Swept Away, which was swamped with customers. Thomasina, who was helping a few older women choose whisk brooms near the fireplace, flashed her eyes at me.

I nodded—message received. She needed help—I just hoped I wouldn't botch sales as badly as I had the other day.

I swept up to a couple, probably in their sixties, who stood near the kitchen brooms. The man scowled behind his glasses. "Yes, I know it's hand-made. But that's still an exorbitant price for a broom."

His wife, presumably, pouted down at the polished wooden handle in her hands and the beautiful flat bristles, sewn with gold and silver thread. "But I *could* use a new one."

"Humph." Her husband shoved his hands in the pockets of his khaki shorts. "We don't need to spend *that* on something that's used to sweep dirt."

I cleared my throat, and they both looked up. I gave them my most charming smile and lifted a palm, frantically searching my brain for a way to close the sale. "They last years, though. It's a good investment."

The wife's expression softened, and she nodded at her husband, who glared at me.

Tough crowd. I cleared my throat. "I'm Laidey, and I work here with Thomasina, who makes these beautiful brooms herself." I swept a hand toward my wiry, white-haired boss. "They're artisan brooms."

He snorted. "They may be, but they're still brooms. And even if that thing lasts us a decade"—he jerked his chin at the broom in his wife's hand—"I'd probably still save money by buying several replacements at Target."

Ooh boy. This was not going well. I floundered about, looking for a counterargument, when Hilde bustled up.

"Oh my! Why, that's a beauty. May I?"

The wife blinked in surprise but handed the broom over to my friend with a smile.

Hilde nodded. "Good weight. And that polished broomstick—'tis a delight for tired hands."

The woman shot her husband a pointed look.

"She's right. And you know my arthritis has been flaring up."

Her husband gave a little nod.

Hilde swept the floor, swaying with her movements. "Why, I feel like a fairy-tale princess's maid with this broom."

I arched a brow in doubt, but the wife nodded. "I had just the same thought." She pointed at the broom Hilde was currently twirling with. "That broom adds a bit of whimsy and fun to otherwise boring old housework." She shot her husband a pointed look. "Which, I might point out, I've been doing *more* than my fair share of for the past thirty years."

He had the decency to look a bit chagrined. As Hilde handed the broom back to the woman with a bow, the husband chuckled. "Oh, why not. It's just a broom after all, not the most extravagant splurge in the world."

Hilde clapped with glee. "Ee! I'm so excited for you, ma'am. You picked a lovely one out."

"Thank you, dear."

The happy husband and wife looked at me, and I swept an arm toward the checkout counter. "I'll ring you up."

As I did just that, I marveled at my friend, who'd moved on to charming another group of customers. She made it look so easy! After I finished with the couple, I rejoined Hilde.

"You're really good at this."

She blinked, her big eyes round. "At what?"

I grinned. "At sales! You're a natural."

She waved it off. "'Tis nothing!"

"Don't sell yourself short. Also, this is your day off." I smiled. "You should be doing something fun—not working more!"

She shrugged. "I like to stay busy. Plus, most of the Faire seems old hat after a few hundred years."

I opened my mouth to ask her some questions about those hundreds of years, when some movement near the door caught my eye. One of the sheriff's enormous troll henchmen filled the doorway, a wooden chest in his arms. He grumbled something, dropped the chest with a crash that startled several of our patrons, then lumbered off.

I rushed to the door and found Mort staring at the chest, tail swishing. "What's this?"

He tipped his little cat face up to look at me. "Apparently, all that is left of Macy Mulligan's worldly possessions."

I raised a brow. "She left them to you?"

Mort sniffed. "She had no last will and testament, so after the sheriff took his share of the estate tax—no doubt *anything* of value—they were so good as to bring the rest to me." He rolled his eyes. "Apparently, I was her next of kin."

Pretty sad when the cursed cat you forced to perform circus tricks was your closest relative.

Thomasina bustled over and muttered, "Can you clear the doorway? This thing's in the way."

"Of course." She hustled off to ring up a customer, and Hilde and I each grabbed a handle of the chest and hefted it up.

"Oof!" We waddled to the other side of the fireplace and dumped it under the stairs with a heavy *thunk*. "What's in this thing? Lead bricks?"

Mort trailed behind, his tail in the air. "Wilt thou open it for me?"

I flipped the latch, lifted the lid, and Hilde, Mort, and I crowded close to peer inside. I took out a dusty old quilt, a pair of cracked leather boots, and then spotted the source of the weight—her rusty cast iron cauldron.

Mort placed his paws on the edge of the chest and surveyed the odd bits and bobs left inside. "Bah. 'Tis worthless stuff."

He meandered toward the door—no doubt to lie in his favorite spot in the sun, where tourists would stop to pet his head. "Do you mind if I look through?" Maybe something here held a clue as to who'd killed Macy.

"Knock yourself out."

A woman who stood nearby browsing jerked her head up and looked from me to the cat.

I shot her sheepish grin and cleared my throat. "Frog in my throat."

She frowned, but eventually lowered her gaze

and got back to shopping. Mort had to be more careful who he spoke around!

Hilde and I crouched over the chest and picked through some knickknacks. I lifted a deck of cards and found a stack of mail underneath. I flipped through the letters and envelopes—most of them coupons from the bread bowl place and other junk mail—but stopped when I found a rolled scroll.

I pulled it open and held the parchment up so Hilde could read, too.

IF THOU DOST wish to keep thy life and limb,
It serves thee well to cease thy show right now.
Allow the Faire's patrons a cultured act,
Or hark! Thou soon shall take thy final bow.

I GAPED AT HILDE. "Someone was threatening to kill Macy!"

She shrugged. "If you say so, m'lady. I never learned to read meself." Her face filled with admiration. "See. I knew you were clever."

I opened my mouth, not quite sure where to start. Alright, I was adding teach Hilde to read to my to-do list. But for now, this was a huge clue.

I shook my head. "I can't believe the sheriff went through Macy's things and didn't think to read this. What a hack!"

And why did something about that note seem familiar?

I jerked my head at the doorway. "Come on—we're taking this to the sheriff, right now!" Halfway there, I remembered I was actually on the clock. I turned to find Thomasina behind the counter, ringing up the last customer.

"Go! I know you're not going to be worth much to me until you clear your name."

I grinned at her and ignored the confused look from the customer. "Thanks!"

Mort lay in the sun beyond the doorway, right in the middle of the lane. Of course he'd cause a traffic jam. Four girls, probably about thirteen years old, crouched around him, cooing and scratching his head and taking pictures with him.

He lifted his head as Hilde and I strode past, the tip of his tail thwacking the dirt. I could practically feel him holding in the urge to yell after us.

With a hiss, he batted the girls away, then trotted over to join us. "I say! Slow down. What's the hurry?"

I shook the letter at him and hoped the thick crowd would make it less obvious I was talking to a cat. "Found a letter threatening to kill Macy in her trunk."

"We're going to give it to the sheriff."

Our march to the jail slowed as we ran into a big crowd gathered in front of the stage.

"Boo!"

"You stink!"

I peered over the heads of the crowd to find everyone's least-favorite elf spouting Shakespeare onstage.

Eldor pressed a hand to his breast and shouted to be heard over the riotous crowd. "Cowards die many times before their deaths; The valiant never taste of death but once."

A dude in the crowd cupped his hands around his mouth and shouted, "I'm dying a thousand deaths from having to listen to your boring speeches!"

The crowd laughed and cheered.

I grinned. I now knew who'd sent Macy that note.

ELDOR GLENHAVEN

I waited until Eldor was inevitably booed offstage, then hurried to follow him. Hilde, Mort, and I ducked through the curtain to the side of the stage, then slowed at the sound of raised voices. We crept closer until we could all peer around the corner.

This time it wasn't Councilor Highbury engaged in an argument with Eldor but a tall, elegant, and *very* pregnant elf.

She wrapped one arm under her round stomach and shook a finger at Eldor with her other. "What am I supposed to do?! I know 'the stage' is your dream, but we'll have another mouth to feed soon!"

Eldor splayed his palms. "I know, dearest, but I am sure that tomorrow's audience will be more receptive—"

Meeeeoooww!

They both looked our way as Mort let out a loud yawn. He shook his head. "Apologies."

I shot him a flat look, then crept around the corner out of hiding, followed by Hilde and Mort.

Eldor frowned. "Excuse me! This area is for performers only."

I'd felt a lot more confident a moment ago, but unease washed over me as I looked at the pregnant elf. I shook it off. Pregnant or not, I was getting to the bottom of who killed Macy.

"Eldor, right? I'm Laidey, and this is Hilde and Mort." I held up the letter. "Does this look familiar?"

The elf scoffed, then peered closer at the scroll. His neck and cheeks flushed pink, and he looked away. "No. I say again, you are not allowed in this area—leave!"

The pregnant elf looked between Eldor and me. "Eldie? What is this little witch talking about?"

I tried not to take that as an insult. I was technically a witch... probably. I stepped my feet wider. "I'm talking about this letter, found among Macy Mulligan's possessions, threatening her unless she stopped her show—to give, I quote, 'the Faire's patrons a cultured act.'"

"I—I—th—that could have been from anyone!" He threw a hand at the other elf. "Tell them, Daria."

Her eyes widened. "Mm-hmm." She nodded, which made the gauzy scarf hanging from her cone-shaped hat flutter.

I wasn't buying it. I leaned into one hip. "It's written in rhyming iambic pentameter."

The two tall elves held absolutely still, and then broke at the same time.

"Dash it!"

"Oof! I told you!" Daria turned to us, her dark brows raised. "I told him—you write it in verse and they're going to figure out it was you!"

Eldor shook his head. "Betrayed by the Bard's signature style."

Hilde shot me a confused look, and I leaned in to explain. "All of Shakespeare's plays are written in iambic pentameter. It's a type of rhythm in poetry." Thanks, Mrs. Brady's senior high school English.

She marveled at me. "I think you must be the cleverest witch I know!"

I grinned and again vowed to teach this girl to read. I turned back to the wide-eyed elves. "Tell me why I shouldn't turn you both in to the sheriff, hm?"

Eldor clasped his hands and dropped to one knee in front of me.

Talk about dramatic. The stage was seriously his calling.

"Prithee! I succor thee to have mercy upon my poor wife and me!"

Daria clasped her hands atop her enormous pregnant belly and grimaced. "Please!"

I held up the letter. "Why did you want Macy's spot so badly that you'd threaten her for it?"

His brows pinched together. "We have a baby on the way."

Mort shot Daria's round tummy a droll look. "You don't say."

"We're barely making ends meet as it is, and now with a child?" Eldor whimpered. "I thought, if Macy's ridiculous Cat and Mouse show was such a hit, imagine how my soliloquies and sonnets would delight and entertain." He looked wistfully up and away. "I just needed a chance to perform during the popular times, not holed away right as the Faire opens!"

Mort snorted. "And how is that working out for thou?"

Eldor's shoulders slumped. "In truth, things are not turning out as I'd hoped."

He and Daria exchanged worried looks.

"Oof!" She winced and clutched her stomach. "Baby's kicking."

Was it? Or was she just trying to play the sympathy card?

I glared at Eldor. "So you killed Macy for her spot?"

Daria choked, and her husband gaped. "Pardon? No! I was simply upset and desperate enough to send her that admittedly ill-advised letter, but I did *not* kill her."

I raised a brow, and Eldor gulped. "I can prove it! I was home all night with my wife the evening Macy died."

Daria nodded. "'Tis true!"

Hm. It was *something*. But I was positive that the pregnant Daria would lie to help cover for her husband. Then again, if they were as poor as they claimed to be, they certainly couldn't have afforded any fairy dust.

I held up the letter. "This isn't for me to decide. I'm handing this over to the sheriff."

Daria hung her head, and Eldor groaned.

"If you're truly innocent, I'm sure you'll be cleared." Well... not entirely sure. *I* was innocent, after all, and was still the sheriff's number one suspect.

Hilde, Mort, and I turned to go, but I had another thought and spun around. "Oh, and just a tip—read the room, ya know? People aren't looking for 'cultured' here." I shrugged. "Fairegoers want to laugh and be entertained. Try some jokes, maybe?"

Eldor frowned. "Jokes? Hm... well, I suppose the Bard himself doth sometimes resort to scatological humor."

I shot him a confused look, but Mort clarified. "Toilet jokes."

"Ah."

Mort, Hilde, and I headed back down the village lanes to the last place I wanted to be—the jail. I had my doubts that Eldor and Daria had killed Macy for her show's time slot, but crazier things had happened. I'd keep my eyes open for another likely suspect, but in the meantime I figured I'd better hand old Watson Boswell the evidence just to be safe.

The two large trolls—I still wondered if they were *truly* trolls or if that was some sort of getup—stepped in front of us and blocked our path until the lazy sheriff waved us in with a yawn. He sat at a wooden table topped with two empty tankards and countless stacks of gold coins.

"You need to make an exchange?" He swept a ring-covered hand at the pile of money in front of him.

"Um… no." I darted a quick glance at the man who sat in the single, tiny cell behind bars. Judging by the plastic Viking hat, striped tank, and board shorts, he was a visitor. He slumped forward, his head nearly between his knees, exposing the back of his lobster red neck. *Yeesh*—that sunburn had to tickle.

The sheriff followed my gaze, then waved a hand. "Don't mind 'im. He's four sheets to the wind—arrested for public debauchery until the close of the Faire or his mates come to collect 'im."

As miserable as the bro looked, at least he got to leave at the end of the day.

The sheriff glared at me. "If yer not here to exchange money, then are you here to turn yourself in?"

Ha! He wished. I handed him the rolled-up scroll.

"What's this?" His eyes widened as he read.

"I found it among Macy Mulligan's possessions."

Mort cleaned his whiskers. "The veritable *treasure trove* your trolls delivered to me earlier."

I raised a brow, feeling pretty satisfied with myself. "I even got the person who wrote the letter to confess to threatening Macy."

Hilde nodded. "She did! She figured it right out."

I had the sheriff's attention. He leaned forward and even from a few feet away I crinkled my nose—he reeked of mead and pipe tobacco. "Who?"

I planted a hand on my hip all sassy like. "Eldor Glenhaven."

It took a moment before a look of recognition registered on the sheriff's face. It morphed into an evil grin. "You don't say." He crushed the scroll in his gloved hand.

"I wouldn't—" I stopped myself from warning him against crushing evidence. Would it really do any good?

The sheriff cleared his throat and gave me a curt nod. "Pleased to see you're at least attempting to be an upright citizen."

I rolled my eyes. "You're welcome." I hesitated. "Just for the record though... I don't really think Eldor killed Macy."

The sheriff scoffed. "Oh my! Well! If *you* don't

think he did it..." He leaned back in his chair and belted out guffawing, wheezing laughs.

The trolls joined him with their slow chuckles. "Huh. Huh."

"Great seeing you again." I shot the sheriff a dry look, then marched back out past the two laughing troll henchmen. I huffed as Mort, Hilde, and I threaded through the crowd back to the broom shop.

I didn't get the feeling Eldor was guilty and was now more annoyed with the sheriff than ever. I hoped handing over the letter to him had been the right thing to do.

"*W*ell done." Thomasina closed the windows to the shop and gave Hilde a nod of approval.

My new friend blushed and dropped her eyes. "Ah. 'Tis nothing." She'd stuck around all day, helping us make sale after sale.

I was about to remind her to not be so dismissive of her talents, when Tom beat me to it. "Psh! Nothing?" The spry little old lady hopped back up on her stool behind the counter. "I wouldn't call a record-breaking day of sales nothing."

I made a mental note to speak to Tom later about hiring Hilde on. She was a natural at selling brooms, the customers loved her, and it was obvious I had no talent for it. With me aiming to apprentice Tom in broom squiring, we—was it too soon to be identifying with the shop like that?—were in need of a good saleswoman.

"Go! You two have worked hard enough today." Tom gave me a gold coin and waved us out the door. Mort stretched, yawned, and then sauntered after us.

"Where to for dinner and libations, ladies?" The tip of Mort's tail twitched. "Prithee don't tell me we're having turkey again."

I nodded my agreement. Not that I didn't love a good turkey leg, but I'd eaten it for breakfast, lunch, and dinner the night before. "I could go for more gyros."

Mort and Hilde exchanged knowing looks.

"What?"

My cat shot me an arch look. "Hoping to run into one handsome pirate captain, mayhap?"

My cheeks grew hot as Hilde linked her arm through mine and chuckled. "Oh, we just tease, m'lady. But me and that cat can both see he likes you and you like him."

Oh geez. Was it that obvious?

As if on cue, we nearly bumped into Bruce as we headed for the gyro line. He shot me his charming smile, escorted us to the back, and once again hooked it up with the gyro guy.

As we all sat around a picnic table, polishing off our delicious, spicy meats and tangy greek salads, I chewed over something I'd been thinking all day.

"The killer would have had to drug Macy with

the fairy dust before she could cast her protective spell around the tent, right?"

Mort nodded. "'Tis the only way they would have been able to gain entry."

I nodded and jabbed the air with my plastic fork. "So… someone Macy came across earlier on the night she died must've slipped it into her food or drink and then followed her back to the tent."

I shuddered, knowing I'd been fast asleep inside while a murderer did their evil deeds.

Bruce licked up a little dribble of sauce from the corner of his mustached mouth. I gulped. Why was that so sexy?

He caught me staring, and I quickly looked down at my nearly finished meal.

"Let's start with the food." Bruce lifted one gloved palm. "Did she eat anything in front of you?"

I shook my head. "No. She caught me at the gates, right at closing, so I don't think she'd had time to eat dinner yet. And then back at the tent, she got all dolled up and said she was heading to the tavern."

Hilde and Bruce snorted.

"What?"

"Let's just say, she wasn't eatin' nothin' at the tavern, m'lady."

Bruce smirked. "Raquel serves a nice, cold pint, but the demon isn't known for her culinary skills."

"Ah." I blinked. "Wait, what? She's a demon?"

Mort, Hilde, and Bruce all stared at me matter-of-factly. I put down my fork and dropped my head into my hands. Just when I was getting used to witches and trolls and fairies, now the proprietress of the tavern was a *demon*?

Mort placed a paw on the table. "Whilst Macy was fond of her liquid dinners, I daresay she would have partaken of some food before a night out."

Bruce finished his bite. "So, we canvass the food stalls and ask them if they served Macy the night she died?"

Hilde nodded, and Mort chimed in, "And then we ask around at the tavern, methinks."

I grinned across the table at Bruce. Maybe it was the romantic twinkle lights strung overhead or the somewhat woozy happiness of being surrounded by happy chatter and delicious smells on a warm summer night, but despite the whole cursed and accused of murder stuff, it'd been a long time since I'd been this happy.

"So you're all helping me investigate now?"

"Of course, m'lady!"

Mort swished his tail. "Methinks thou hast a rather small chance of succeeding otherwise."

Bruce winked. "I can take a short break from my poetry to help a fair damsel in distress."

I arched a brow. "Distress, huh?"

He chuckled. "I concede your point. You have this well in hand... though you must give me the 'fair' part."

My cheeks grew hot, and Hilde bumped my knee with hers under the table.

After we finished off our gyros, Bruce, Hilde, Mort, and I split up to ask around with each of the food vendors. We all came up short—no one remembered serving Macy that night. Which left only one place to check…

I curled my lip as we headed toward Ye Olde Bread Bowl, the name sounding even less appetizing now that I knew the rumors about customers finding hair and mouse droppings in their food. "Do you really think she ate here?"

Hilde wrung her hands. "Would be odd, wouldn't it? Seein' as her ex and his new wife run the place."

We headed to the window, but the shutters were closed and all the tables in front empty—even of those two creepy twins I'd seen chowing down the other day. We walked around to the back of the stall and found the door to the kitchen open. Though the heavenly scent of fresh bread wafted out and my mouth watered, I reminded myself not to be fooled —*mouse droppings, remember, mouth?*

I crept up to the kitchen and peered around. Voices sounded from the next room over—the one the ordering window opened to. I probably only had a few seconds, so I scoured the place for clues. Hot embers and half-charred logs glowed in the bread oven on the far wall. Bags of flour, sugar, and salt lined a shelf over the butcher block counter, and various pots and pans hung from a rack overhead. A bunch of utensils, including several rolling pins, stuck out of a ceramic container next to the sink, and beside that an open tin glowed.

Wait a second!

I glanced back at Bruce, who stood right behind me. "What's that?" I pointed at the square tin, its lid on the counter beside it. Golden light spilled out, with the powder inside sparkling. It looked a whole lot like Macy's—

"Fairy dust." A middle-aged man with thick gray hair and a close-cropped white beard came around the corner and startled me. He replaced the lid on the tin.

I jumped and pressed a hand to my heart.

He wiped his hands off on a striped kitchen towel, then tossed it over his shoulder.

"What's going on?" The woman who'd served me the other day hurried around the corner and froze when she spotted Hilde, Bruce, Mort, and me. Her eyes grew round, and she seemed to shrink. "What's this?"

The man glanced back at her, then turned to us with a brow raised. "What can I do for ya?"

I smiled in what I hoped was a friendly way. That poor woman looked terrified. "Are you Kip?"

He nodded and leaned his hip against the counter, crossing his ankles. "I am Kip Mulligan, and this is my wife, Nell."

The meek woman inched behind him.

Interesting that Macy had kept Kip's last name.

"What's this about then? We're closed for the night."

"We, uh—we were wondering if Macy Mulligan ate here the night she, uh… died." Was the death of his ex a touchy subject? Did he still care for her? Hilde had told me they fought like crazy, but still, I wanted to be respectful in case he was mourning.

Nell's eyes grew wide as Kip's grew hard. "Who's asking?"

I gulped. "I'm Laidey, and I'm trying—"

"I know who you are! You're the one accused of murdering my ex-wife!"

I waved my hands. "I didn't, though. I'm trying to figure out who the real killer is and was hoping you could help."

Nell and Kip both studied me for a long moment before he gulped and looked down. "Yep. Macy came by here. Had a bowl of chowder."

"Weird."

Kip frowned at me. "Why?"

I hadn't really meant to say that out loud. I shrugged. "Just… well, you're her ex-husband, right? Was that not a bit strange?"

Nell huffed, but that was the only sign she had anything to say on the matter. She stayed half-hidden behind Kip, her pale lips pressed tight together.

"Nah. Macy came by here quite a lot. She liked my bread bowls." He smirked, a little twinkle in his eye.

Nell pressed her lips into a flat line. She seemed a bit upset by this. Then again, it probably wasn't easy having your husband's ex hanging around all the time. Especially not when she was Macy Mulligan.

"So she ate here. Did you notice anything strange about her? Was she with anyone?"

Nell shook her head along with Kip. "Nah. She ate alone and seemed like her normal self."

Bruce raised a thick brow. "Any idea where she went afterwards?"

Nell sniffed and looked away, and Kip smirked. "Most *every* night you could find her pints deep at the pub."

I nodded—that jived with Mort's impression, also.

I patted the doorjamb. "Well, thank you for your help." My eyes drifted to the tin of fairy dust. "Uh, can I ask why you have a tin of fairy dust?"

Kip's eyes darted to Nell behind him, and he snorted. "It's for the mice and critters that come in. We've had our fair share of rodent problems lately."

Nell flashed her eyes at him, and Kip's grew wide as he seemed to catch himself. He waved a palm at me. "Don't let that get around, mind you. We've lost enough business from it."

Nell huffed and shook her head.

"But Nell here doesn't have the heart to poison the darned things, so we got some fairy dust." Kip pulled his lips to the side and grumbled, "Even though it's ten times as expensive as poison would be."

Nell peeked around Kip's shoulder and spoke for the first time in a small, high voice. "We just put them to sleep and rehome them."

Hilde and I exchanged small smiles. That was sweet of them.

"Thanks again for your help."

Mort, Bruce, Hilde, and I left the bread bowl place and headed for Wilde's Abbey.

Bruce shook his head. "They have fairy dust and served Macy Mulligan the night she died. Easily could've been Kip and Nell that put some in her food to make her drowsy."

I nodded. "True. Though, if they can barely stand to hurt mice, would either of them really have had it in them to kill Macy?"

Hilde hmmed. "Nell, no. But what 'bout Kip?"

He seemed more likely to have done it to me, too.

"Still does not explain how either of them would have gotten ahold of a Viking sword, though."

I nodded down at Mort. "Fair point."

I hoped we'd get some better answers at the pub.

THE TAVERN

$\mathcal{B}$ruce, Hilde, Mort, and I squeezed into the crowded Wilde's Abbey. My ears buzzed with the hubbub of laughter, conversation, and lively bagpipe music blaring from the corner stage. Bruce, a good head taller than Hilde or me, rose on his toes and looked around. He bent his mouth close to my ear. "No chance of a table, I'm afraid."

I cupped my hand to my mouth. "That's okay! Let's get some drinks and make our rounds!"

He nodded and led the way, while Hilde scooped Mort into her arms to keep him from getting trampled. Though patrons crowded up to the bar, Bruce immediately grabbed Raquel's attention. My pirate captain friend seemed to get VIP service everywhere he went.

She sidled up with a mischievous smirk on her

full lips and the flames from the fireplace reflecting in her eyes. As she took the drink orders from Bruce, I shuddered as I remembered that she actually was a demon. Maybe those flames weren't just reflections...

We soon had cold draughts in our hands (I carried Hilde's for her since she had her arms full with Mort) and milled about. A group of men and women with scarves on their heads played a heated game of dominos near the fire, while several tall, elegant elves who reminded me of Eldor and his wife Daria sipped from glasses of wine.

Once again, the Viking clan had taken over the long table in the middle of the pub. The leader with the horned helmet sat in the center, nearly doubled over with bawdy laughter, pounding the table with his fist. It set the tankards rattling and only made the other Vikings laugh harder. Bo Erikson, one of my top suspects, sat at the leader's side. He laughed along too but had that strained look of someone who didn't quite get the joke.

I looked at my new friends and jerked my head toward Bo and the others. We threaded through the packed crowd of fluttering fairies, arguing dwarves, and grunting trolls until we hovered near the Viking table. I leaned back and eyed Bo's hip—still no sword. While I suspected that the sword in Macy's chest was probably Bo's, I still had serious doubts that the young man had killed her, in spite of his bragging that he had.

Maybe if I confronted him in front of his buddies, something would shake loose.

I waited for a break in the booming laughter, then slid closer to the table. "Hey Bo!"

The skinny guy looked up and blinked at me from behind his glasses. It took him a moment to place me, but once he did, he scowled. "Hey."

The Viking beside him, an older guy with a red bushy beard and deep lines etched into his face, winked. "Well now, Bo, aren't you going to introduce us to your pretty friend?" His eyes drifted to Hilde, still holding Mort like a baby on his back. "And *her* pretty friend?"

Bo's throat bobbed. "Er… this is Laney?"

"Laidey." I extended my hand to the Viking, expecting him to shake it, but he held it and pressed a scratchy kiss to the back of my hand.

"A pleasure." His eyes lingered on mine.

Yikes! I smiled and extricated my hand as quickly as possible. I flashed my eyes at Bruce, expecting him to share in the joke with me, but instead I found him unusually serious. His dark, nearly black eyes bored into the Viking.

I cleared my throat—this was going well so far.

I thumbed at Bo. "I met Bo the other night. He was telling me all about how he'd killed Macy Mulligan." I planted a hand on my hip and shot him an "oh, you rascal" kind of look.

The red-bearded Viking slapped Bo so hard on the back that he folded forward over the table and wheezed out a cough. "We had our doubts about this one, but the boy's proved himself worthy of being a Viking!" He thumped his chest and a few Vikings near us lifted their tankards and barked out, "Skol!"

I nodded and lifted my own beer in cheers. "Skol. Totally." I turned back to the red head. "So... why'd you have your doubts? Didn't think Bo was blood-thirsty enough?"

He nodded. "Exactly. Look at 'im. Nothing but skin and bones." He threw a thick, calloused hand at Bo, who actually looked like he wanted to murder *me* right about now. "He failed all our initiation tests and was frankly about to be ousted from the clan." He shook a finger at Bo. "But the boy had us all fooled, he did! Went and killed, all by himself!"

I sucked on my lips. "Wow. You must be so proud."

He nodded. "Couldn't be more so."

Bo shot daggers at me. "Was there something you wanted or...?"

I leaned into one hip and tried to play it casual. "Yeah, see, it's silly, but Sheriff Boswell..." The Viking growled, and I nodded my agreement. "Real piece of work, that sheriff, but see he thinks *I* killed

Macy and now I've got to find the *real* murderer so he doesn't hang me."

The red-bearded Viking nodded along, sympathetically. "Well, you've found him!"

"Hm. True, but..." I shot Bo a puzzled look and played dumb. "It's just that, when I asked you about Macy's tent the other night, it was almost like you'd never been inside it. Which I know is crazy, because whoever killed Macy *must've* been inside the tent."

The older Viking looked from me to Bo, a deep crease between his bushy brows. "What's she saying?"

Bo shifted in his seat and couldn't quite meet my eyes. "It was dark. Whatever."

"Hmm. Right, but it got me thinking. If you *did* kill Macy, you wouldn't mind confessing to the sheriff, would you? It'd really help me out, and I'm sure you'd be able to answer all his questions, like how you got around her protective spells."

I shot him a pointed look, and Bo's thin chest heaved. "I—I don't think that's necessary."

The older Viking scoffed. "The lady is asking you to clear her name." He thumped his chest again. "Besides, any true Viking would be proud to claim a kill. Blood and bravery, brother!"

I spun to face Bo and thumbed at the older guy. "Yeah. Blood and bravery, Bo." I raised my brows high. "So you'll come talk to the sheriff with me?"

He bared his teeth. "Now's not good."

The older Viking shot him a curious look. "Now that I think of it, how *did* you get around the witch's spells?"

Bo's throat bobbed and he leaned away from the massive man beside him. I decided to float a theory I'd been forming.

"Call me crazy, but I was thinking—don't you have a reputation for being forgetful, Bo?"

He paled as the older guy nodded. "Forgot his cleats the other day for toga-honk." He scoffed as I looked to Bruce for clarification.

He leaned close, his voice low. "Basically tug-of-war."

"Ah."

I turned back to Bo. "Interesting. I also was wondering why you chose to leave your sword in Macy's chest? Did you forget to take it with you?" I scrunched up my face. "Seems odd, seeing as one's sword is pretty important to you Vikings, isn't it?"

The older guy stroked his beard, his beady eyes narrowed on Bo, who squirmed. "That is odd. Why *did* you leave it, Bo?"

Our interrogation had caught the interest of a few others who sat nearby and now eavesdropped.

Bo looked around wide-eyed at them all. "I—I—"

I clicked my cheek. "You know, it almost makes me wonder if you left your sword somewhere, and the *real* killer nabbed it and then used it to murder Macy and frame you for it."

Bo's mouth fell open, and the Vikings nearby leaned forward, their eyes trained on the young guy, the tension palpable.

"I—I have to go to the bathroom!" Bo leapt to his feet and disappeared in the crowded pub before anyone could stop him. I felt a little bad about putting him on the spot like that, but then remembered how lame it was to brag about killing someone. Even someone as nasty as Macy Mulligan.

"Ooh, you did scare him good!" Hilde beamed, and Mort gave me an approving nod. Bruce still glared at the red-headed Viking who now conferred with his clan members.

"Think he did it?"

"I think he may be taking credit for someone else's kill!"

Gasp!

While the Vikings mulled over Bo's guilt, I felt more confident than ever that my theory was correct. Bo had left his sword somewhere, and the real killer had scooped it up and killed Macy with it. Bo had just seen an opportunity to prove himself to his clan by taking credit for it. I pulled my lips to the side. Unless he'd been so desperate to fit in, that he'd actually gone ahead and murdered Macy.

He'd been here the night she died and could've slipped fairy dust into her drink. But still—why wouldn't he brag about doing that? And why leave his sword in her chest?

"Pssst! Hey—new girl. Pssst!"

Hilde, Bruce, and I whirled toward the sound of the voice. A pale, unkempt man in the starred robes and pointy hat of a wizard urgently waved us over to his booth, where he sat alone. "Hey! Make like a tree and split over here!"

"That maketh no sense," Mort quipped. His head lolled off Hilde's arm, his little paws limp. Man, he was spoiled.

I shrugged at Hilde and Bruce, and then we laced through the crowd over to the wizard. He scooted to one end of the green leather booth. "Slide in! Quick!"

I glanced around, unsure of the need for haste, but slid in behind Bruce, followed by Hilde.

The old man leaned forward, his pale blue eyes darting wildly from side to side. "I hear you're asking around about Macy Mulligan?"

I raised a brow. "Do you know something?"

"Oh." He chuckled, his laugh raspy. "Oh. I know something, alright."

Bruce looked him up and down. "Care to share?"

The wizard jumped. "Oh! Right." He pressed a hand to his chest, his knuckles covered in strange, rune-like tattoos. "Creet, the Putrid."

"Ah, yes." Bruce pointed at him. "You're the wizard who invented those foul-smelling fireworks a couple years back."

Creet double-clicked his cheek. "That's me, baby." He leaned forward, and his white, scraggly beard dipped into his tankard. "Listen up. The night Macy died was a wild one. Drinks, dancing on the bar, a conga line of gnomes!"

I shot Bruce a questioning look, and he frowned and slowly shook his head. He mouthed, "High on fairy dust," then jerked his head at the wizard.

Right. I crossed my arms. So, probably none of that happened.

"Then, out of nowhere, Macy gets in this fight with a fairy!" Creet's pale eyes grew round. "It was nuts!"

I raised a skeptical brow. "What'd this fairy look like?"

"Blond hair, wings, about yay tall."

Hilde rocked Mort like a baby. "That could've been Poppy, m'lady."

I nodded. It was unclear how much of Creet's story was fact and how much was fairy-powder-induced hallucination, but it was worth looking into.

"Thanks so much."

We scooted out of the booth, but just before we left, Creet snapped his fingers. "Oh! And she was on a date."

I hesitated. "With who?" Macy had put on some serious blush and freshened up before she went out that night. At the time, I'd suspected she was meeting someone.

Creet waved a hand airily about. "I dunno... some guy with a beard."

So that narrowed it down to almost every man in the Faire. We waved our thanks, then moved off. Though Creet the Putrid seemed pretty out there, it might be useful intel.

Who had Macy fought with? And who was the bearded man she'd been on a date with?

THE ENCHANTED FOREST

While finishing our draughts, we decided the best course of action would be to visit the Enchanted Forest, where the fairies hung out. We hoped to figure out which one had gotten in a fight with Macy... assuming, of course, that Creet the Putrid wasn't totally off his rocker and made the whole thing up. If I had to guess, my money would be on Poppy.

After Bruce picked up our tab (quite gentlemanly of him) we all wound through the Faire's lanes in search of answers. And Mort even walked on his own four feet this time.

"Ooh! The Enchanted Forest." Hilde shimmied her shoulders with glee. "They're all so glittery and sparkly with their delicate little wings."

Bruce leaned close on my other side and lowered

his voice. "Best to be on high alert in the presence of the fairy queen."

I lifted a brow.

"She doesn't answer to the same laws as the rest of us. While you're in the Enchanted Forest, you're in her realm, and her word goes. So best to stay on her good side."

I frowned. "Okay…"

We reached the entrance.

Bruce gave me a tight-lipped smile that made his thick mustache twitch. "Best of luck in there."

I gaped at him. "You're not coming in?"

He scratched the back of his neck and looked away. "Remember that part about staying on her good side…"

"This doth not bode well." Mort sat his thick haunches down as he waited for Bruce to explain.

His cheeks grew pink. Was the pirate captain actually blushing? I fought a grin.

"Magnolia—she's lovely—but she took a fancy to me a few decades ago, and though I tried to politely turn down her advances… well, let's just say she does not take kindly to rejection."

Hilde raised a blond brow. "She is a lady used to gettin' her way."

Bruce touched a finger to the side of his nose. "You'll have your best chance of staying on her good side if I stay out of it altogether."

I chuckled a bit as we left him at the gate, and Hilde, Mort, and I wound our way through a lush, tree-lined stone path. After a couple of twists and turns, the streets of the Faire were out of sight and the huge trees shading the area blocked all view of the buildings and tents. It really did feel like we'd wandered into a forest.

Fireflies—or maybe fairies in miniature form?—floated around the tree trunks and the dulcet notes of a harp drifted through the warm night air. We took a turn at a large stone and stepped into a magical sight.

Fairies and mermaids lounged around a lagoon, moonlight reflecting off the rippled surface. A mermaid with blue hair stroked the strings of her harp, and the one who had to be the fairy queen, Magnolia, sat on a throne made of petals and vines, surrounded by fawning fairies. The petals were clearly made of plastic and the boulders fake, but in the moonlight the attraction was strikingly convincing.

I spotted Poppy Lacewing right away. She lounged on the edge of the pool, kicking her feet in the water with her hippie buddies. She looked up as we entered and scowled.

Another fairy, with a lavender bob and a tiny upturned nose, flitted in front of us. "Greetings."

"Oh, uh—greetings." I gave an awkward little wave.

"Greetings," the rest of the mermaids and fairies murmured.

Wow. It was really pretty here. And also pretty creepy.

"Do you seek an audience with our fair Queen Magnolia?" She blinked her huge, vacant eyes. "The stars must be shining in your favor. Normally, our fair queen would have retired after her last photo op to our inimitable Fairy Kingdom, but tonight Her Highness had a royal craving for cheesy fries, so we've stayed late within the public realm of the Enchanted Forest." She waved her hands airily about at the attraction. "Lucky you, she's available now if you wish to speak with her?"

I leaned to the side to look around her fluttering wings. Queen Magnolia picked at her nails, her luscious pink locks blowing like she had a fan in front of her. I bit my lip. Maybe that was a spell I could use.

Hilde nudged me, and my attention snapped back to the fairy who hovered in front of us, with a sweet—though empty—smile on her face.

"Right. Um... not necessarily. We just heard a fairy had gotten into a fight with Macy Mulligan at the tavern a few nights ago, and were hoping to have a word with whoever that was?" I raised my voice and glanced past her gossamer wings, hoping someone would pipe up.

Gasps and worried murmurs sounded around the lagoon.

The fairy queen glared across the water at me. "What does this witch say, my forest children? That one of us has been fighting?" Her teeny tiny baby voice sounded like tinkling bells—and also totally forced.

Poppy Lacewing jumped to her feet, shot me a murderous look, and then composed her features into the picture of serenity and turned to her queen. "I believe this witch is mistaken and quite possibly drunk."

"Hey!" I planted my hands on my hips. Slightly buzzed, *maybe*, but that was irrelevant.

Poppy ignored me and continued. "I believe she has been misinformed about a calm, composed conversation Macy Mulligan and I had."

The queen arched a brow but waved a delicate palm dismissively. "See that you clear up this witch's misconception then. We can't have outsiders thinking we're anything but peace-loving children of the forest."

The mermaid with the harp strummed as if to accentuate the queen's decree.

Poppy bowed low, then spun to face me and gave me a terse jerk of her head. She drifted over, led us back down the lane toward the Faire, and once out of sight of the lagoon, huffed.

"What in the shell do you think you're doing?!" She stomped her tiny, bare foot.

I leveled her with a flat look. "Oh, drop the act, alright, we're not in front of your queen cult leader. I have a witness who saw you get into a fight—*not* a calm discussion—with Macy Mulligan at Wilde's Abbey."

Poppy clenched her jaw, her nostrils flared. "Fine! We had an argument, okay?"

I crossed my arms and raised a brow. "About?"

She huffed and looked toward the thick ferns lining the path. "I *might* have tried to liberate Macy's animals from her abusive confines the night before, and she figured out it was me somehow—one of her protection spells, no doubt. When she confronted me at the tavern, I admitted to it."

"You were trying to steal the cat and mice? Why?"

Mort scoffed. "I daresay I think I heard you skulking about outside the tent!"

Poppy shot him an exasperated look. "I was *trying* to help you!" She looked at me. "To set them free. They deserved to be free and wild and live their lives!"

I frowned. No one had seen or heard from the mice since Macy's murder. Pretty sure "free and wild" wasn't working out for them.

Poppy huffed. "I just can't stand to see animals injured or eaten or used for tricks! But I couldn't even get past her spells to get into the tent, so it's whatever."

Hilde grunted. "I have to agree with you, miss, but isn't there a better way than to steal the animals?"

Poppy snorted. "You mean like go to the sheriff? A whole lot of good that'd do!"

Couldn't argue with her there. I wondered how many shenanigans happened as a result of the Rennies feeling like they had no recourse but to take the law into their own hands.

"Didst thou kill Macy to free us?" Mort's tail swished side to side.

"What?! No!" Poppy jutted out her jaw. "I don't condone violence of any kind. We're peace-loving creatures here."

Right. "Except for attempting to break and enter?"

Her cheeks reddened in the moonlight.

"Alright, so if you didn't kill Macy, then where were you that night when she died?"

Poppy rolled her big eyes. "Not that it's any of your business, but if it'll stop you ruining my reputation with my queen... After I ran into Macy at the tavern, I was so upset, I flew around for a while to calm down before returning to the Enchanted Forest."

"Was anyone with you?"

Her eyes grew wide before she composed herself.

"Do you mean, do I have an alibi? No, okay. I was by myself. Just—just drop it!"

She marched off back toward the lagoon.

"Huh. So Poppy has no alibi, was acting squirrelly, had the motive of freeing Mort and the mice, and had the means—the fairy dust to drug her."

Hilde nodded as we meandered back toward the Faire and Bruce, who was waiting on us. "She admitted to being at the tavern with Macy—she could've drugged her drink."

Mort curled his tail. "Plus, Poppy admitted to trying to breaketh into Macy's tent, which means she'd discovered the protective spells and would've *known* she had to drug Macy before the witch had a chance to cast them."

Those were all good points.

Another thought occurred to me. Poppy had been at the tavern—at the same time as Bo Erikson. She could've nabbed his sword from him, and being as forgetful as he was, he probably would've assumed he'd misplaced it somewhere. It was the perfect way to frame him and draw the attention off her.

I still didn't have absolute proof, but Poppy Lacewing had just become my top suspect.

A FORBIDDEN LOVE

The next day I spent most of the quiet morning studying broom making with Tom as a few customers filtered in and out. She had me help her sort the broom corn by length and thickness. Though I often caught my mind wandering, I did my best to focus on learning a new skill. And, though it was fairly tedious, it still felt good to be doing *something* productive. Months sulking on the couch had not been good for my mental health.

Just after lunch, a ruckus in the square drew my attention. Thomasina looked up too, but without me having to say a word, she waved me away. "Go."

I grinned. "How did you—"

"You're incredibly nosy." She looked at me over the rim of her glasses. "I know you won't be able to focus until you figure out what's going on."

I hopped off the stool and strode toward the

door, where Mort lounged in a patch of sun. "I prefer to think of myself as curious."

Tom snorted. "You know what they say about curiosity killing the cat."

"I beg your pardon!" Mort lifted his head and blinked his green eyes at my boss, who just shook her head.

The cat rolled to his feet and trotted after me as I headed toward the big, raucous crowd gathered in front of the stage. As predicted, Eldor was reciting his Shakespeare and the audience was having none of it.

"Boo!"

"You suck!"

"Vern would take that as a compliment," Mort quipped. I shot him a grin, then rose on my toes to look over everyone's heads.

The riotous mob quieted slightly as a newcomer marched on stage from behind the curtain. I raised my brows—had Sheriff Boswell suddenly taken up acting?

Eldor stopped midspeech, his eyes round. "What's this?"

"You're under arrest, Eldor Glenhaven." The sheriff placed his fists on his hips and stepped his booted feet wider. His two troll henchmen waited below the stage.

"For—for what?" The panicked elf glanced all around, like a caged animal.

I had a sinking feeling in my stomach that this had something to do with the threatening letter I'd handed over to Boswell.

Suddenly, the curtain beside the stage swished, and Councilor Highbury joined the fray. He waved his hands, shot the now rapt crowd an appeasing grin, then turned to the sheriff. "I know he's terrible, but surely it can't warrant arresting him!"

The crowd chuckled, and some dude yelled out, "Huzzah!"

"Arrest him!"

"My ears are bleeding! That's a crime!"

Eldor didn't seem to know which way was up. He spun from the sheriff to the amused crowd to the councilor. Seemingly in a fit of desperation, he cleared his throat and attempted to return to reciting sonnets.

"All the world's a stage; And all the men and wom—"

The sheriff grabbed Eldor by the ruff around his neck and dragged him back.

"YECK!" He let out an exaggerated choking noise, and the crowd laughed.

"Wait! Wait!" As the sheriff dragged Eldor toward the steps by his collar, Councilor Highbury grabbed his ankles and fought to pull the lanky elf back. "I admit, his acting is an assault on the senses, but that can't be nearly as bad as an actual physical assault!"

The crowd laughed harder as the sheriff and

councilor fought over Eldor, who, with his doublet half-pulled over his head, flailed his arms.

"What's going on? Pick me up!" I crouched down, scooped Mort into my arms, and then held the heavy cat up so he could see.

My heart went out to poor Eldor. I didn't think he'd killed Macy—I was nearly convinced it'd been Poppy! This was my fault.

A wheezing, hacking sound made me spin Mort around to face me. I found my cat's eyes squeezed shut and his mouth open.

"Are you laughing?"

He nodded, laughing so hard he couldn't breathe. "It's—quite comical!"

I made an indignant noise, then turned my attention back to the stage.

"He's a murderer!" The sheriff shouted to be heard over the raucous laughter.

"You're telling me his act was so bad it actually *killed* someone?" The councilor, shocked, released Eldor's ankles, which sent the sheriff and elf tumbling backwards, down the stairs, until they collapsed in a heap at the base of the stage.

The crowd howled.

Eldor sprang off the stunned sheriff, looked around, then sprinted off. He didn't account for the two nearby trolls, who stuck their thick, scaly arms out and clotheslined him. Eldor's feet flew off the ground, and he landed flat on his back in a puff of dirt.

"Hnnggghhh," he groaned.

I giggled as the crowd lost it. Okay. Yeah. It was kind of funny.

The two trolls hauled Eldor to his feet, and the disheveled sheriff shook a finger at him. "Eldor Glenhaven, you are hereby arrested for the murder of Macy Mulligan."

Eldor paled, then fainted, and the sheriff and trolls marched him across the square toward the jail. The crowd applauded and whistled and cheered them on.

"This is all horribly ironic." Mort shook his head, and I couldn't entirely suppress a snicker.

I shook myself. Not funny! A man just got arrested for murder, and it was probably my fault. I replayed the way Eldor had landed on top of the sheriff, crotch to face, and giggled again.

I was a terrible human.

I felt even worse as Eldor's pregnant wife, Daria, waddled straight toward me through the dispersing crowd, her eyes blazing. "You!" She jabbed a finger at me, and I held Mort in between us as a feline shield.

"You turned that letter in to the sheriff, didn't you?" Her chest heaved, and her pointy cone-shaped hat sat askew on her head.

I nodded slowly. "I did. Calm down, I'm not sure it's good for you to get excited in... you know... your condition." I dipped my gaze to her enormous pregnant stomach.

As if on cue, she winced and groaned, clutching her tummy.

Oh lordy, was she going into labor?

"Urg." She gritted her teeth, held up a finger, and a moment later, straightened somewhat. "I—am giving birth—any day now." She bared her teeth, her eyes boring into mine. "You clear my husband's name so that he can be present for the birth, or so help me I'll—" She doubled over again, wincing in pain.

I saw that as a good time to make my exit. "You okay? You good?"

She glared at me, and I scampered off with Mort still in my arms. "Do elves have special magic? Can she hex me?"

My cat just chuckled.

I sprinted after the sheriff and his trolls and caught up with them a few minutes later, just outside the jail.

"Wait!" My chest heaved as the sheriff and trolls spun around, the unconscious Eldor still slung between them.

"Ah! Lemonade!"

"It's Adelaide."

The sheriff gave me an approving nod. "Thank you for your assistance. Thanks to you, we have caught the scoundrel who killed Macy Mulligan."

I shook my head, still trying to catch my breath. Clearly, Mort wasn't the only one in need of more exercise. I swallowed. "It's not—Eldor—I think—Poppy Lacewing is the killer and—"

The sheriff leaned close, smelling all sweaty and boozy, and winked. "You're officially cleared. Case closed. Eldor Glenhaven is taking your place in the trial tomorrow. Let it go."

He and the trolls dragged Eldor inside the jail while I just stood there, watching. Being cleared should've felt good, liberating. Instead, it just felt like I had a brick in my stomach.

I hung my head and groaned. "I messed up, big time." I slunk over to a bench, and Mort sprang up to sit beside me. I slouched down and huffed. "Great. I got a probably innocent elf arrested, leaving his pregnant wife to give birth by herself."

Mort nodded. "Don't forget that they are poor. They said they can barely make ends meet, dost thou recall?"

"Ugh!" I dragged my hands down my face.

"Plus, once the sheriff's done with him, Daria will likely be a widow."

I sat upright. "We can't let that happen. We can't. That's just too messed up." I clenched my hands into fists.

Mort's tail swished from side to side. "What art thou going to do about it?"

I nodded. "I've got to prove Eldor's innocence by

proving Poppy did it... probably." I shrugged. "I've got to find the real killer, and I suspect it's that shady pet-snatching fairy."

Mort nodded as a few girls blowing bubbles skipped by. "How to prove it, though?"

I jumped to my feet. "We'll just—we'll go talk to her again. I'll tell her about what happened to Eldor, and maybe she'll feel so guilty she'll just confess."

Mort snorted as he hopped off the bench. "That's likely."

"Well... it's all we've got. Let's go."

After checking for Poppy at the Enchanted Forest and then the hippie fairy hangout near the tents, we came up empty. All her fairy pals claimed they hadn't seen her for a couple of hours. I'd given up and was headed back toward the gate to the main fairgrounds, when Mort meowed and got my attention.

"I daresay! Look!" He stared down at the dirt path that wound through the grassy field.

"What?" I didn't see anything.

He rolled his eyes, then patted the dirt with his little paw. "Ere we call it quits, I say have a look at this sparkly stuff."

I crouched down beside him and cocked my head. Huh. Now that he mentioned it, there were quite a lot of glitter on the ground.

"It's a trail!" Mort trotted along the dirt path,

then darted into the grass, following the glitter the whole way. I jogged to keep up.

"Do you really think this is significant? It's probably just glitter."

"Nay!" Mort called. "I recognize this glitter—and scent. It's Poppy."

I raised my brows. "Seriously?"

He jogged over to the Viking clan's tents and stopped. "It leads in there."

I frowned. Why would a trail of glitter lead to the Vikings? They certainly didn't use it.

Mort and I crept into the camp, which was empty this time of day, past the fire pit and small pile of animal bones, following the glitter until it stopped at the flaps to a brown tent.

Mort and I leaned our ears close to listen to the muffled voices coming from inside.

"I just think you're the—the fairest fairy in all the Faire."

Mort rolled his eyes. "Everyone doth think they art a poet." To my shock and horror, he dashed into the tent.

"Mort!" I hissed.

"What the—?"

"Get out of here!"

A moment later the tent flaps flew open, and Mort zipped out, faster than I thought him capable of moving. He dashed behind my ankles, and I looked up to find Poppy Lacewing and Bo Erikson standing side by side.

My jaw dropped. "Poppy?"

Mort sniffed. "Told thou I recognized her scent."

The fairy's long locks were tousled, and her bright pink lipstick was smeared all over Bo's lips and cheeks. I gasped. "You two are together?"

"Grrr!" She balled her tiny hands into fists and stomped her bare foot. Her wings buzzed so quickly they actually lifted the angry fairy an inch off the ground. "Why won't you leave me alone?!"

Bo looked from his angry girlfriend to me. "She's been bothering you too? That's the witch who ruined my street cred with the Vikings!"

I rolled my eyes. "Do you seriously want to earn the respect of dudes who give you 'street cred' for killing someone? Get some better role models."

Though she still had her shoulders hiked up to her ears and her face was bright red, Poppy lowered back down to the ground and shot Bo an arch look. "She does have a point."

I planted my hands on my hips and glared at them. "Why didn't you tell me you were together?" I drew a circle at them with my finger. "Why all the secrecy, huh? Did you two plot to kill Macy?"

I glanced around. Though the Viking camp appeared empty, it was broad daylight. These two wouldn't attack me now... would they?

"Huhhhh." Poppy slumped her shoulders and looked to the sky. "You're so annoying! I'm a pacifist—a child of nature, peace loving." She flashed her eyes at me. "Get it, dummy? If the other fairies found out I was dating a Viking? I can't even…" She shook her head.

"No good, huh?"

Bo snorted and adjusted his glasses. "Yeah, and like, I'm trying to seem all tough and violent so I can fit in with these Viking dudes." His eyes grew round. "I mean… they're pretty scary. If they knew I was dating a fairy, I'd be kicked out of the clan in a heartbeat."

They turned to face each other, their eyes full of nothing but each other.

"It's a forbidden love," Poppy murmured.

As their lips slowly drifted together, a piece slid into place for me. "So—you two were together the night Macy was killed?"

They both jumped as though they'd forgotten Mort and I were here. Oh, young love.

Bo gulped and Poppy lifted her chin. "Yes, we were." They clasped hands.

"Fine." I waved it off. "I don't care, except that you now have alibis." And I'd lost my top suspect. Unless they'd worked together to kill Macy? But these two could barely keep their hands off each other. Somehow I found it difficult to imagine them masterminding a murder.

"Get a tent," Mort called as we wandered away from said tent.

"You know—"

I turned at the sound of Poppy's high voice.

She poked her head out the tent flap. "If you're serious about finding Macy's killer, I saw her with her ex that night at the pub."

I frowned. "Kip?"

She raised her brows, then ducked back inside.

Huh. Kip *did* have a beard... could he have been the man Creet the Putrid saw Macy with? But they were exes... who by all accounts didn't get along. I doubted they'd been on a date like the disheveled wizard said, but he could easily have gotten that part wrong.

I bit my lip. Kip *did* have access to fairy dust. Had he been there to kill Macy that night in the pub?

MICE

*M*ort and I hustled back through the Faire. I probably needed to get back to work at some point. Then again, Tom knew I had to see this through and find the killer before I could concentrate on my apprenticing. Before, it'd been about clearing my name and staying out of the hangman's noose. Now, I needed to make sure the sheriff arrested the right person.

I decided to explore that little tidbit Poppy had dropped about seeing Macy and Kip together at the pub. Though I'd already taken my lunch, it was still midday and the lines were long around the food court. Since I was starting to know my way around, I ducked down the shady alleyway Bruce had used to cut to the back of the gyro place.

I glanced back at my cat as we picked our way around crates and bags of trash. "I know it doesn't

185

necessarily mean anything if Kip and Macy talked at the pub, but he made it sound like they—"

"AHHHHH!"

High pitched shrieks made my heart nearly jump out of my chest. I gasped and stumbled back, nearly tripping over Mort, as the two white-blond twins I'd seen eating outside the bread bowl place yelped and ran frantically in looping circles. With my pulse pounding in my temples, the little boy and girl ducked behind a crate, then peered at me over the top of it.

I muttered to Mort out of the corner of my mouth. "What's with these two?"

My cat scrunched up his brow. "I do not know. They seem familiar, though I cannot seem to place them."

I cleared my throat. "Uh—you two okay?"

As one, their blond, bowl-cut heads rose until they stood, shoulder to shoulder, facing me. My mind couldn't help but go to the twins in *The Shining*, and I shuddered but tried not to let on how creepy I found them.

"You startled us." The boy's buck teeth stuck out. The girl wrung her hands at her chest. They both stared at me, unblinking, their expressions blank.

Cute kids.

Mort and I edged around them in the narrow alley. "Sorry about that. You actually startled me too."

The girl stared at me from under heavy brows. "We do that sometimes."

They both talked in a breathy, singsong way that made me suspect they were plotting my murder.

"I bet. Hey, are your parents around here somewhere?"

"No."

"They're gone."

Sad. Also, so crazy creepy.

Mort jerked his head toward the other end of the alley. "Besteth not to press them on this. Thou wouldst be surprised how many odd and vile creatures disguiseth themselves as children—from ghosts, to demons, to—"

"Alright, I'm sold." I gave the kids a quick wave and a "Watch out for gnomes," then booked it out of the alley after Mort. I shuddered again, glad to be back in the sunlight, then made my way with Mort over to Ye Olde Bread Bowl.

Like usual, the tables out front were empty—aside from a few Faire patrons eating gyros and turkey legs from other food stands. With no line, I walked right up to the order window, but neither Nell nor Kip were manning it, so we walked around to the kitchen door in the back. Once again, it stood open.

Kip, who manned the stove, and Nell at the sink looked up as we approached. Kip dragged a sleeve across his moist forehead and walked up to the doorway, wiping his hands on his apron. "Good day. How met?"

Mort nodded. "Fine, fine. Good day to you, sir."

I glanced around, making sure we weren't alone and isolated, just in case this was Macy's killer we were talking to. Plenty of kitchen doors stood open all around us, letting in some air in this humid midday heat.

"We wanted to ask you some more questions about Macy."

Nell, who'd been washing dishes, stilled and looked at her husband with wide eyes.

He shrugged, though his face reddened. "Yeah? What about?"

I raised a brow. "I was wondering why someone saw you at Wilde's Abbey with her the night she died?"

Kip's eyes grew round, and his face and neck turned red and blotchy. He strode toward us, shooing us away. "You know, now's not a good time."

I raised a brow. "You busy? Because there's no line out front."

Kip's chest heaved. He glanced back at his wife, then licked his lips and lowered his voice. "Might be best if we speak elsewhere."

I narrowed my eyes. "Why? You have something to hide?"

He scrubbed his beard and mouth, then half-turned to Nell. "Well, honey, I know I said I wasn't feeling well that night and I had to head home and leave you to man the place, but I just thought one pint wouldn't hurt so—so—I—I, uh—"

Nell raised a gentle palm to silence him, then, with a hanging head, sidled forward. She shot her husband a significant look, then turned to me, grim. "He was there at the tavern to confront her."

Kip stared at his meek wife like he'd never really seen her before. Even I was a little gobsmacked that she'd interrupted.

"She doth speak," Mort muttered.

She sucked in a breath through her nose and lifted her weak chin. "Macy was the one ruining our business." A muscle in her jaw jumped. "She—she kept slipping her trained mice into our kitchen to get hair and droppings everywhere and then fed the rumors about it." Nell pressed her lips tight together and frowned.

Kip gaped at her. "Nell, I don't—"

She held up a palm again, stopping him. "It's time we told the truth."

I frowned. "Do you have proof?"

She nodded, somber. "I caught her mice before. Recognized them. I had a feeling they weren't mice, same as this cat isn't really a cat."

"Well, I s'pose it is a gray area. I am a man enchanted into a cat."

Nell shrugged. "It's why I used the fairy dust to put them to sleep and return them to the outside.

Couldn't bear it if I accidentally killed some poor innocent people." Her face reddened. "Though clearly Macy had no problem with setting them loose in our kitchen and putting them in harm's way."

Her husband placed a hand on her shoulder, and Nell stiffened. "Honey, I'm sure Macy just knew what a mild, soft heart you have and that you couldn't have brought yourself to kill a fly."

Nell pressed her lips tight together.

"Why was Macy doing this?"

Nell sniffed. "She couldn't accept that Kip had moved on with me—she was trying to ruin us."

I narrowed my eyes at Kip. "And you went to confront her about this?"

His throat bobbed. "Er… yeah…"

Nell huffed through her nose. "I tried to tell the sheriff about how she'd been sabotaging our business, but he didn't do anything."

No surprise there.

"So… yes, Kip went to confront her."

I arched a brow. "And how'd that go?"

"Uh… w-well… we, uh… talked."

"Riveting," Mort muttered.

I got the feeling Kip was hiding something. "Did she admit to letting her mice loose in your kitchen?"

"Oh! Uh… um…"

Once again, Nell stepped in. "You said you had

some words, right? And she denied everything, got sleepy, and went home?"

Kip frowned. "Yes. Yes, she did get quite sleepy."

I planted a hand on my hip. "Did you drug her?"

"What? No!" He shook his head. "No, nothing like that."

I exchanged a dubious glance with Mort. So, his awful ex was sabotaging his business, and they just discussed this calmly over drinks and then everyone went their separate ways?

Likely story.

But I nodded. "Alright. Well, thank you for being honest with me." That line was my mom's trick to guilt me into confessing anything I'd been holding back on when I was a teenager.

I raised my brows and looked from Kip to Nell, lingering in case they had something to add.

"Alright, well, farewell." Kip tipped his head, and he and Nell got back to work while Mort and I looped back around toward the front of the food stalls.

"Something seems fishy there. Did Macy get sleepy because Kip added some fairy dust to her drink, then followed her back to her tent and stabbed her?"

Mort nodded. "He had access to fairy dust and was at the pub with Macy."

"And he clearly had a motive—Macy was ruining him and Nell financially with her mice and rumors."

As we rounded the corner, I was startled to see someone actually waiting in line for a bread bowl. "Bo?"

The scrawny guy looked up, then his expression soured as he recognized me. "Oh. You again."

I pasted on a bright smile. "No Poppy?"

He looked around, then hissed, "Not in public!"

"Right, sorry." Mort and I walked closer.

He leaned in and whispered, "Parted ways after you and your cat barged in. Can't be seen eating together."

I frowned as I realized he was going to be Ye Olde Bread Bowl's sole customer. "Do you eat here often?"

He grinned as he scanned the menu hanging above the order window. "All the time."

I raised a brow. "You're not bothered by the rumors then? About mice droppings in the soup?"

He scrunched up his nose. "Nah. Their potato soup reminds me of home."

I felt a pang of sympathy for Bo. He looked to be in his early twenties, at the oldest, and Raquel had mentioned he'd only been trapped in the Faire for a couple of months. Poor guy—he must still be adjusting, just like me.

Something tugged at my mind—something prompting me to ask more questions. "Did you eat here the night Macy was killed?"

He rolled his eyes. "This again."

"Did you?"

He huffed, but looked off like he was thinking. "No. I had a salad that night." He shrugged. "Poppy's trying to get me to go vegan."

I nodded. Huh. If Kip had killed Macy, he would've needed to get ahold of Bo's sword.

"Be honest—when did you first notice your sword was missing? Was it the night Macy died, or earlier?"

Bo shook his head. "It was a couple days earlier, alright? Me and Poppy have been sneaking off to get some alone time together, and I figured I just left it somewhere."

I nodded. "Do you think you ate here the day you lost your sword?"

He shrugged. "I dunno. Probably. I eat here every day."

"Thanks, Bo."

Mort and I headed toward the broom shop as Nell hurried up to the window to take Bo's order.

"What art thou thinking?"

I glanced down at my cat. "I'm thinking, if Bo eats at Ye Olde Bread Bowl every day, Kip could easily have had a chance to nab his sword—the kid is so forgetful."

"Yes, likely." Mort lifted his tail high. "Methinks thou art onto something."

I nodded. "I think Kip killed his ex-wife to keep her from sabotaging his business and harassing him and Nell. I can easily picture Macy Mulligan doing something like that, and I bet Kip and Nell were at the ends of their ropes after the sheriff wouldn't do anything to help them."

"You think Nell was in on it, too?"

I thought it over. "No. She's so gentle and meek—she couldn't even kill the mice, after all. But it did seem like she was defending Kip in there. I bet if she hadn't been around, he would've caved under pressure and confessed."

I grinned. Which suddenly gave me an idea for how we were going to catch Kip and get all the evidence we needed to have him arrested and Eldor cleared.

BAIT

*M*ort and I outlined a rough plan to catch Kip, then pitched it to Thomasina. She graciously allowed us to use the broom shop as the location for our sting.

"Just try not to wake me up," she grumbled. "And nobody better hurt any brooms."

After we closed up shop, Mort and I met up with Hilde and Bruce and filled them in over corndogs and mead.

"First of all, brilliant plan." Bruce's dark eyes twinkled under his thick brows. "First-rate skull-duggery."

I grinned back at him.

He held up a gloved finger. "Though, it occurs to me that a young woman, such as yourself, and a cat, may not be a match for a cold-blooded killer."

Mort snorted. "Do *not* underestimate the damage

a cat canst do. Remind me to tell you the tale of my epic battle with the Cat of Palug someday."

I smirked. "Is this some kind of alley cat rumble?"

Mort narrowed his green eyes. "This was a fight celebrated in song, for your information, back from my time as a human man." He puffed up his furry, black chest. "The kitten's mother was a magical swine, and that feline felled no less than one hundred and eighty of my soldiers—strong men, all of them—before I dispatched it."

"Riiiight." I flashed my eyes at Mort. "So this epic battle involved a grown man fighting a tiny kitten, whose mother was a pig?"

Mort huffed. "'Tis truth. All of it!"

Sure it was. "Did it have 'nasty, big pointy teeth'?"

Mort nodded, emphatically. "Yes, it did in fact!"

My reference to the killer bunny from *Monty Python and the Holy Grail* was lost on him. Though, thinking of the movie, why did it somehow remind me of Mort...?

Bruce cleared his throat and brought me back to the matters at hand. "To be clear, I have nothing but confidence in your independence and strength—but what I'm proposing is that I join your plan to provide backup. You know—the muscle to your brains."

I smirked and exchanged a look with Mort. "We were actually planning to ask you to join our stake-out, so I appreciate that. Thank you."

Hilde swallowed a bite of her corndog and looked at me with round eyes. "May I come as well, m'lady?"

I raised a brow, surprised. "Of course, but... you're sure you want to? It might be dangerous, and I know you've already worked a long day."

She smiled, a little twinkle to her eye. "I dunno... sounds kind of exciting to me."

It was settled.

I looked around at my trio of new friends. I may be cursed to spend eternity in an enchanted Renaissance Faire, but it wasn't all bad. "Thank you all for helping."

As we finished our meals, Daria, Eldor's very pregnant wife, slid past, a meager portion of fries in her hands. Her expression was drawn, and she looked like she was about to pop. I gulped and felt even more determination to catch the real killer tonight and free Eldor in time to be by his wife's side for their baby's birth.

After dinner, we reviewed the plan, then sauntered over to Ye Olde Bread Bowl. Bruce and Hilde hung back, out of sight, while Mort and I went up to the order window. It took a few moments before Nell realized she had customers, but she bustled over, her brow pinched.

"Have you thought of more questions?" She eyed me warily.

I put on a bright smile. "Just one. Could we speak with Kip, actually?"

The color left her face, but she nodded, then shuffled into the kitchen. A moment later, Kip stomped over, shaking his head. "What is it now?"

I looked past him, to the left, and spotted Nell eavesdropping from the kitchen. Oh, well. It was fine if she heard. Maybe the pressure of his wife asking questions would only help propel Kip into doing something desperate. And a desperate reaction was what we were banking on.

"Just wondering—Nell mentioned that she suspected the mice were actually people Macy had bespelled, right?"

He shrugged. "So what?"

"Well, when Macy was killed, the mice were in the tent, yes?"

"I guess."

"And after she died, if she *had* enchanted them, the spell would've been broken?" Mort and I had talked this point over with Thomasina earlier. She'd agreed that was the case, but of course, we weren't sure if the mice were actually people, or that Macy had been the one to enchant them if they were. If it had been someone else's curse, they would still be mice, just like Mort was still a cat.

But we were hoping Kip didn't know any of that.

He frowned, eyes narrowed. "I suppose so. Why?"

I nodded, slowly. "You suppose? So... you haven't run into the mice-turned-people yet?"

He grew still, his voice gruff. "What are you getting at?"

I leaned forward, my voice deadly quiet. "Well, *I* have. I found them, and they witnessed the murder. They told me who killed Macy, and they're willing to testify."

Kip's face reddened. "Wha—What's that got to do with me?"

"I think you know. The former mice and I are going to the sheriff tomorrow. I'll give you until then to do the right thing." I shot him a significant look, then glanced at the kitchen where I caught Nell watching. She jumped and ducked back behind the doorway.

Good. The pressure was on—from me, and I was sure Nell would be peppering him with questions.

I nodded at the red-faced Kip, then spun on my heel, and Mort and I marched away.

Fingers crossed he'd take the bait.

I SNIFFED, grunted, then blinked my eyes attempting to adjust to the dark. I frowned, not recognizing the strange, deep shadows around me. Where was I?

My brain fog cleared a bit.

Oh, yeah. A stakeout in the broom shop. We'd

turned out all the lights and were waiting for Kip to break in and attempt to silence me before I could go to the sheriff. Mort, Hilde, Bruce, and I huddled together behind one of the massive shelves of brooms. Apparently, I'd fallen asleep, and I wasn't the only one. As my eyes adjusted to the dim moonlight, I realized that dark lump by my feet was the snoozing Hilde spooning Mort. No shocker, my lazy cat was also out cold.

Had Bruce kept watch?

I stilled. I'd fallen asleep—on Bruce's beefy shoulder! Yay! But, oh no! I'd drooled a bit. I lifted my head and turned to him, wincing. "Sorry, I think I got a little spit on—"

He pressed a gloved finger to his lips, then jerked his head toward the window.

Suddenly, I realized what must have woken me up in the first place. A dark shadow hunched on the windowsill, and the pane creaked as it eased open. We'd left it unlocked, hoping Kip would discover this as an easy way in. After all, I didn't want Tom to have to dock my wages to pay for a broken window.

Looked like our plan was panning out exactly as, well, planned.

My heart raced—for more than one reason—as Bruce held an arm around my shoulders, our eyes locked on the dark shadow of the intruder. The pirate captain gave me a gentle squeeze, then slowly, silently pulled his arm back and rose to a crouch, a shuttered lantern in his hand.

A dull thud sounded. Then silence.

I gulped. Even my swallows sounded loud right now. I turned wide-eyed to Bruce, who gave me a reassuring nod.

He was a pirate captain, I reminded myself and my racing heart. This wasn't his first experience with skullduggery, as he'd put it.

The floorboards creaked, and Bruce held up a finger. We waited. More footsteps and quiet creaks sounded as Kip crept toward the stairs.

Bruce counted down with his fingers and I felt like my heart stopped.

Three... Two... One...

Bruce and I leapt to our feet, he unshuttered the lantern, and I yelled, "Halt!"

I guess all the old English was starting to wear off on me.

The intruder froze as the lantern light spilled over the room. As my eyes adjusted, I realized the shape was wrong.

This wasn't Kip.

Hilde and Mort startled, gasped, and jumped to their feet. Hilde brandished a broomstick. "Where is he?"

Bruce huffed beside me. "Where is *she*, more like it."

Thin, meek Nell stood in front of the dark fire-place like a deer caught in the headlights.

A deer with a sharp dagger in her hand.

I gaped, gobsmacked. Nell was the killer? *Nell?* The woman who couldn't even use poison on mice had murdered Macy in her sleep and was clearly planning to do the same to me? I shuddered. I was never sleeping again.

Mort—with more agility than I thought the chubby cat capable of—sprang up atop a rack of brooms. "Is this a dagger which I see before me? Where art thou going with it, Nell Mulligan?"

That seemed to snap her out of her stupor. She sprinted for the open window.

A CONFESSION

*a*s Nell sprinted for the window to make her escape, some instinct kicked in, and I tore past Bruce after her.

"Adelaide—wait!"

I didn't have time to respond to the pirate—or rethink what I was doing. As Nell climbed out the window, I grabbed the skirt of her long dress and yanked. She tumbled backwards—taking me with her.

"Oof!" The wind was knocked out of me, and I struggled to catch a breath, which was difficult with Nell flailing on top of me.

"Let go!"

I realized from her shrieking that in the fray I'd managed to grab ahold of a clump of her light brown hair.

Suddenly, the room lit up with bright, golden light just before Bruce skidded to a stop above us. He kicked the dagger further away from Nell's flapping hand, and it slid away with a *clang*.

He then pinned Nell's wrists together and dragged her off me.

"OWWWW!"

Oh shoot. I'd forgotten to let go of her hair. I now held the clump in my hand.

Mort sauntered over and looked down at me, nearly nose to nose. "Nice souvenir."

"Eck!" I shook my hand and dropped the hair, then lurched to sit up.

Hilde dropped down beside me. "Are you alright, m'lady? That was mighty brave of you."

"And foolish," Mort added. "You do realize we art all trapped here in the Faire? 'Tis not as if she could have escaped."

"Oh." I curled my lip. "Right."

As Hilde gently put an arm around my shoulders, Bruce wrestled with Nell. He strained to keep her arms pinned to her sides as she balked and kicked.

"Oh, stop yer thrashing." I glanced over my shoulder as Thomasina tromped down the stairs in a long white nightgown and matching sleep cap. She snapped her fingers, and Nell went limp.

Bruce had to dip down to catch her before she slid to the ground, her head lolling. Her frantic eyes still blinked and darted around, though.

"What have you done to me, witch?"

Tom jerked her chin at a wood chair in the corner. "Put her there."

As Bruce dragged Nell over, Tom approached. She pulled her glasses onto her nose and looked her over with mild surprise. "Nell, huh? Didn't think you had it in you."

Nell's normally meek, stoic face was now transformed by rage and panic. She curled her lip in disdain. "No one did! That's why Macy never saw it coming."

Tom turned to me as I shakily got to my feet with Hilde's help. "You okay?"

I nodded and winced at the pain in my hip. "Just a few bruises; won't kill me."

Tom's concerned eyes swept over me before she nodded. "Good. I told you not to wake me up, though."

"Sorry."

She winked. "Eh, I can sleep when I'm dead. This was worth it."

Bruce, his dark eyes full of concern and broad chest heaving, marched over and gripped my shoulders. He looked my face over, then the rest of me. My cheeks grew hot.

"You're not injured?"

I shook my head, a little too flustered to speak.

He pulled me into a tight hug, warm and strong. *I could stay here all night.*

Then pushed me away again, holding me at arm's length. He gave me a stern look. "What possessed you to tackle a known murderer with a dagger?"

I shrugged. "I'm not sure. It just looked like she was getting away, so I ran after her."

"Brave and clever." Hilde clasped her hands together and looked at me like I was her hero.

Bruce shook his head and, judging by the slight quirk of his mustache, was torn between disappointment and amusement. "Have you heard the saying 'discretion is the better part of valor'?"

I chuckled. "Yeah. Guess I forgot the discretion part."

Bruce released my shoulders—much to my disappointment—then turned to Tom. "Will you be alright while I summon the sheriff?"

The tiny old lady in her nightdress waved him off. "Go—I've got this in hand." She narrowed her eyes at Nell in the corner.

The pirate captain nodded, and on his way out leaned close. "I don't approve of you risking your life like that, but I have to admit, it was impressive. I like the cut of your jib."

He winked, and my cheeks grew hot. After he ducked out the door, Hilde, Tom, and Mort all shot me arch looks.

"What?"

Tom just snorted.

Bruce returned a few minutes later with a disheveled, grumpy sheriff, two groggy trolls, and Kip.

"Nell!" Kip rushed to his wife's side. "Why can't you move?"

Nell, who currently looked like a puddle of a human, glared at Tom. "The witch put a spell on me."

"And I'll take it off once you're safely behind bars." Tom crossed her arms and returned the glare.

Ooh, you go, Tom. I was happier than ever to be this powerful witch's apprentice. I was sure I could learn a lot from her.

Bruce thumbed at Kip. "Figured it'd be best to round up all the key players."

I nodded my agreement.

Kip spun to face all of us, his brow wrinkled. "What's this all about then, eh?" He stood beside his slumped wife, one hand on the back of her chair.

Ol' Watson Boswell glared at me. "Yes. Do tell."

Oh, so now he was annoyed at me for having done his job? I took a breath and squared my shoulders. *Discretion, Laidey, discretion.* Probably best not to get even further on the sheriff's bad side.

"We caught Nell sneaking into the shop with this." I handed the sheriff her dagger. "I have no doubt that she intended to murder me in my sleep, just like she did Macy Mulligan."

One of the trolls gasped.

Kip gaped at the dagger, then rounded on Nell. "That was my grandpa's. Nell!"

"Oh, shut it!" A surprising amount of venom came from the slumped-over woman. I shot Tom a grateful look. Thank goodness she'd magically immobilized her. "You were running away with her!"

Kip inched away from his wife and rubbed the back of his now beet-red neck. "Well... we can't *run away...* we are all trapped here..."

"So you admit it! You were leaving me for that wench, Macy Mulligan!" Nell's wild eyes shot daggers at Kip. "You were married to that awful woman once; didn't you learn your lesson then?"

Kip looked like one of those dogs people film after they've done something naughty. Like when the trash is upturned and strewn all around the house, and the dog is cringing, tail tucked, but still trying to maintain its innocence.

He lifted a palm, unable to meet her eyes. "Yeah, but, she's a witch, honey, she probably used her charms on me and—"

"Charms my hat, you lily-livered, beetle-headed son of a knave!"

He gulped, his shoulders hiked up as far as they'd go. "We just had history, you know?"

"This!" Nell directed her gaze at the rest of us. "This is the cowardly, cheating husband that drove me to madness, along with that dusty old wench Macy."

Kip cringed.

"Macy had been harassing me and our restaurant for months! Spreading rumors, sneaking her mice in to torment me. And then this?" She glared at Kip. "On top of it all, she was cheating with you and practically rubbing it in my face."

I looked down. I knew how *that* felt. It'd been rough since Chad left me for his sidepiece. I could sympathize with Nell's pain—but that was about it. I mean, I'd had a few revenge fantasies, but none of them involved actually stabbing Meredith to death. And I'd certainly not gone and done it!

The sheriff gawked from Nell to me, back to Nell. "So you admit it? You killed Macy Mulligan? But... how?"

"Cracking detective work, this." Mort rolled his eyes.

I nodded at my cat.

Nell bared her teeth. "I overheard from Poppy about the protection spells on Macy's tent. So I got ahold of some fairy dust—pretended it was for the mice—and slipped some into her soup when she came to dine that evening."

Kip covered his mouth.

"Bo had left his sword behind a few days prior, and I'd stashed it away, just waiting for the right opportunity. I knew it'd throw everyone off the trail and point them Bo's way."

She glared at her husband. "You thought I was

such a fool. Like I wouldn't figure out that when you said you were sick—leaving me to work our business all alone—you were actually sneaking off with *her*! I followed you two to the pub, waited until she staggered back to her tent, and then snuck in."

She huffed at me. "Imagine my surprise to find someone else in the tent, but you seemed out cold, so I left well alone. I see now I should've killed you when I had the chance."

I shuddered. Yep. Definitely never sleeping again.

"I stabbed Macy, and I'd do it again too! She was a menace, breaking up happy households!"

Yeah. Nell and Kip seemed *super* happy.

I planted a hand on my hip. "And you followed me here tonight to kill me before I could turn you in to the sheriff?"

"That's right." She glared. "I overheard you tell Kip you'd found the mice people and they'd been witnesses to the crime. I planned to force you to tell me where the former mice were. Then I was going to kill them too, and make it look like you'd attacked them and then the lot of you had all ended up dead in some big struggle." She looked to the raftered ceiling. "I dunno. I was improvising that part a bit. I figured it didn't matter much—sheriff's not exactly known for his hard work."

Boswell blinked. "Hey."

I smirked. "Well, joke's on you, Nell, because I actually have no idea where the mice are."

Mort frowned. "Why dost thou always look at me when thou sayeth that?"

Oops.

"Urg!" Nell—still slumped in the chair and unable to move—grunted with frustration. "Why did you have to be such a pain? I was going to dispatch you and leave it at that. You're new, no one would've even missed you."

Ouch.

Bruce slid closer to me. "That, I'm afraid, is gravely untrue."

Hilde nodded. "Aye! She's my friend."

Aw.

Tom glared at Nell, then turned to the sheriff. "Boswell, please get this refuse off my property."

He glared at Nell. "With pleasure." He jerked his head, and the trolls lumbered up to Nell, picked her up between them—one holding her shoulders, the other her feet—then shuffled out, with Kip trailing behind.

"A drink to celebrate? And ease our nerves?"

I nodded gratefully at Bruce. "Yes. A thousand times, yes." My hip ached, my heart pounded, and I felt like I'd just taken my last final exam—totally deflated. I needed some grog—stat.

Hilde grinned. "I'm in."

"I shall join thee." Mort licked his paw and cleaned his whiskers.

I turned to Tom. "Care to join us?"

She grinned but waved us off, already shuffling to the stairs. "You young kids go enjoy yourselves." She pointed at me and winked. "Don't go too crazy, we've got yoga in the morning, remember?"

I groaned, and Tom chuckled her way upstairs.

HUZZAH!

The next day around noon, after a morning of flubbing more broom sales, I turned to Thomasina. Having solved the mystery of Macy's murder, I now felt it was time to address some of the other issues I'd been mulling the past few days.

"Tom?"

She looked up from her broom crafting.

"I've been giving this a lot of thought. You know my friend Hilde? She's hardworking, a natural saleswoman, kind and—"

She held up her hand and cut me off. "She's hired, if she wants the job."

I grinned. "Really?"

She nodded. "If I've got you as an apprentice, we'll need someone on the floor." She sniffed. "And frankly, anyone would be better than you, but I agree. Hilde's gonna make me a fortune." She winked.

"Thank you!" I moved to hug Tom, then hesitated. "Is it okay if I hug you?"

She rolled her eyes but beckoned me on with her hand. I squeezed the tiny woman, then beamed at her. "Can I go tell her now?"

Poor Hilde was probably slaving away at another twelve-hour shift in that sweltering turkey leg stall. She'd spent way too long paying her dues, and it was time she got a chance to prove what she was capable of, as she'd put it.

Tom nodded. "Go on. I'll man the shop."

I hopped off the stool beside her, then froze and turned back. "Wait—did you say I'm your apprentice? Like... officially?"

Tom nodded. "Yes! Now that you've cleared your name, I hope you'll be able to concentrate better."

I grinned. "Thank you!" As I headed toward the door—and Mort lounging in the sun outside it—I was surprised at how happy that made me. I mean, it's not like I grew up dreaming of becoming a broom maker someday. But I liked Tom and this adorable shop and was looking forward to a new challenge. It'd be interesting and fun to learn a new craft and get to work with my hands again. As world-rocking and bizarre as it was to be stuck in the Faire and discover I had magical powers (still left to be explored), it was also kind of exciting.

After my breakup with Chad, I'd had a down-ward spiral and hadn't realized, until the last few days, how much I'd isolated myself and pulled back from life. But now I had a new friend in Hilde, a mentor, a talking cat sidekick, and—I blushed just thinking about it—a potential romantic something with Bruce. It really didn't even matter if he returned my crush or anything happened—it just felt good to have those fluttery feelings again.

As I stepped into the bright midday sun, I glanced down at my cat. "Hey, Mort—you want to come with me to tell Hilde the good news?"

He peeled a green eye open, then rose on his elbow. "Doth this errand involve turkey legs?"

I grinned and nodded. "You know... I think it might."

He was on his feet faster than I thought the chubby cat was capable of. As we walked across the square, we ran into the thick crowd gathered in front of the stage, and I reflexively tensed. But instead of boos and airborne cups of beer, the audi-ence was... laughing?

I frowned and looked at the stage.

"Didst Councilor Highbury finally give Eldor the boot and replaceth him with a popular act?" Mort, who had no chance of seeing over the crowd's heads, looked at me.

My eyes widened. "Nope. That's Eldor up there."

I dipped down and scooped up Mort, then held him up Simba-style so he could see.

The lanky elf half climbed the curtain, shouting Shakespeare. "Cowards die many times before their deaths—"

"I said get down!" Councilor Highbury—who was apparently now part of the act—tugged on the elf's curled-toe shoe, trying to pry him off the curtain. "Your act is an assault on the ears!"

Eldor whirled to face him. "And your face is an assault on the eyes!"

The crowd laughed, then howled as Eldor's shoe slid off his foot and Councilor Highbury fell and did a backwards somersault off the side of the stage.

I raised a brow in concern, until I saw him hop to his feet, and both he and Eldor mug at the audience, clearly tickled by all the laughs and applause they were getting.

This went on for another five minutes—the schtick was Eldor trying to put on his boring Shakespeare act while Highbury, playing the enraged stage manager, tried to drag him offstage. It all resulted in a lot of laughable insults and some pretty genius slapstick.

"Art imitating life," Mort muttered.

After Highbury finally managed to drag Eldor offstage, I hugged Mort to my chest and slapped my thigh, clapping along with the thunderous applause. They burst out of the curtain and took their bows, hand in hand. As the audience dispersed, I caught Daria—with a newborn wrapped in a sling against her chest—collecting tips in an upturned feather hat absolutely bursting with bills. As I got closer, my eyes widened—a lot of them were twenties.

I shifted Mort onto one hip and beamed at the smiling Daria. "Congratulations!"

She looked tired but happy. "Thank you." She gazed lovingly down at the wrinkly, pointy-eared baby against her chest. "Gave birth to him last night —we're calling him Dardor. It's a combination of Daria and Eldor."

I kept my smile plastered on. "Oh... it's... nice."

She shot me a flat look.

Oops. I had the worst poker face.

Eldor and Highbury sauntered over, all smiles. Eldor embraced his wife, then cooed over his newborn.

"Congrats, new dad!"

He nodded at me and Mort.

"Thank you." He slid an arm around his wife's shoulders. "And thank you for getting me out of jail last night—it was just in time to make the birth of our little Dardor."

I waved it off. "Don't mention it." Especially since I was the one who probably got him arrested in the first place... I shot Highbury a grin. "Looks like your new show is a hit!"

Eldor scoffed like he couldn't believe his good

luck. "Yeah, you know, if you hadn't gotten me arrested, I'd never have had the inspiration."

Er… yeah. "Glad to help."

Daria glared at me.

"You know, all these years, I've managed from the side stage." Highbury pulled his hat off and dabbed at his balding head with a kerchief. "But my! It's thrilling to be *on* it! I wasn't sure I had it in me when Eldor approached me about joining his act, but gads! They loved us!"

"They did. Well, congrats all around!"

We left the new parents and the jubilant Councilor Highbury and headed for the turkey leg stand. We joined the back of the long line, only to realize I recognized those fairy wings and that shaggy hair at the table beside us.

"Bo? Poppy?"

They looked up from their greek salads.

The fairy raised a brow. "In line for a turkey leg?" She scoffed.

Bo pointed at his salad with his fork. "You know, you should really try going vegan. It's plenty delicious."

"Actually, we're in line to speak with my friend Hilde, who's working up front." They didn't need to know that two turkey legs were also in Mort's and my future.

Poppy looked arch, but somewhat appeased.

Mort and I shuffled a step forward. "So... you're out in public together?"

Bo nodded. "I realized I'll just never fit in with the Vikings. Poppy's convinced me to pursue a nonviolent way of life."

"Oh, good. Your pillaging days are behind you."

Poppy made eyes at Bo. "And I realized that I just have a thing for bad boys."

I sucked on my lips to keep from blurting out that Bo was about as far from a bad boy as they got. I had a good guess from his thin limbs and pale skin that Bo's life before being trapped in the Ren Faire had probably involved a lot more video game battles than real life fights. Which frankly was a lot more appealing to me —it was just funny the way Poppy saw him. But hey— that was a good thing about starting over here. We all got a chance to be who we wanted to be, a fresh start.

I waved and wished them well and shuffled forward. We were here to help Hilde get her own fresh start.

As we moved on past another table, I recognized the weird twins sitting nearby. No bread bowls this time—pretty sure Kip had a lot going on today, what with Nell being formally charged for murder. The kids each had a turkey leg in hand, nibbling furiously at it like corn on the cob. They looked like mice, holding each end between their mitts—

"Oh. Oh no."

Mort looked up at me with questioning eyes, and the person in front of me in line glanced back. I tried to give a pleasant smile but was pretty sure the shock was written all over my face. Since we were too close to regular humans for Mort to talk, I gently brought him up over my shoulder, then lowered my voice.

"The two creepy twins?"

Mort grunted.

"They're the mice!"

My cat jerked his head up, whipped around to look at the pale twins who'd once been white mice, then started laughing so hard he wheezed. The guy in line looked back again, brows pinched, and I scrunched my nose. "Hairball."

He turned back around as I muttered to Mort, "Get it together."

Frankly, I found the realization a lot more creepy than it was funny. I mean, who knew how long Macy had these two kids trapped as mice? Where were their parents? And what monster had given them those tragic bowl cuts? My anxiety for them was somewhat allayed when an older couple in peasant garb joined them at the table and doled out milkshakes for everyone.

Good. Someone had taken the creepy kids under their wings. Then again, Macy had claimed to do the same for me. But that was an issue to look into another time.

We finally shuffled to the front of the line, and Hilde gave us a strained smile from the other side of the counter. "Welcome to— Oh! M'lady and Mort!" She dipped down as she curtsied. "Come for some turkey legs?"

Her blond curls clung to her damp forehead, and her cheeks flushed in the heat. Behind her, open flames flashed in the grill, and the cook yelled something at another worker.

I had to get her out of here.

"No."

Mort hissed.

"I mean, yes, two turkey legs please... actually make it three, you hungry?"

"Ha!" She flashed her eyes. "Starving. But I don't get a break for another six hours."

I grinned. "Actually, I talked to Tom, and she said she'd like to hire you on as a saleswoman."

Hilde's face went slack. "What?"

"You were amazing the other day—a natural. What do you say? You want the job?"

She blinked. "Am I dreamin'?" She pinched herself and winced. "It's real! Oh, m'lady!" She clasped her hands and beamed at me. "You are too kind!"

I waved her off. "It's really Tom."

"Give me just a sec!" She held up a finger and dashed to the back as the line behind us grumbled. She and the cook exchanged words, he started shouting, and she yanked her apron off. Hilde nabbed three orders of turkey legs and ran out the side door with the cook still shouting at her.

"Let's go!"

I ran, still holding Mort, to catch up with her. I glanced back at the now empty order window. "What happened?"

"I told the cook I quit and to keep my wages for the day to pay for these turkey legs." She giggled. "He was mighty angry, but truth is, he's mighty angry about everythin'." She shrugged. "Place is fully staffed today—someone else can take over. I'm not workin' there another minute."

I glanced back as we threaded through the crowded lunchtime tables. Indeed, a young man stood at the order counter, and the line moved up.

We snaked our way off the main streets of the Faire to a secluded little area and sat in the grass in the shade of a big tree.

As we munched our turkey legs and celebrated Hilde's new job, Mort demanded she tell her quitting story again—in detail. Apparently, he loved a good quitting story.

"One day I shall regale thee with mine. 'Tis a doozy."

I frowned at my mysterious cat. "Okay. Sure."

As Hilde chatted happily, giddy with excitement, I leaned back against the tree trunk and took stock of the moment. This was my life now.

While I was going to work on developing my magical powers—if I indeed had some—and figure out a way to break this curse, in the meantime it wasn't so bad.

Hilde held her turkey leg up and snapped me out of my reverie. "Cheers to new friends and new jobs. I feel like the luckiest wench in the world."

We were going to work on Hilde not calling herself a wench, but for now, it was time to celebrate. I held up my turkey leg and tapped it against hers, like clinking glasses, then tapped Mort's in his little paper tray.

"To new friends and new jobs!"

And a whole new life… that I was actually kind of excited to explore.

"Huzzah!"

End of Book 1

Want more lovable leading ladies, clever twists and turkey leg-sized laughs?
Curl up with ***All Swell That Ends Spell***, the next book in the Magical Renaissance Faire Mysteries!

The fun continues at the Faire!
Keep reading and don't miss a single mystery.
Read the entire magical series from authors Erin
Johnson, Trixie Silvertale, and Nova Nelson.

What happens when a wicked witch gets whacked?
Find out in *Much A'Broom About Nothing*.
What happens when a mermaid is murdered? Find
out in *All Swell that Ends Spell*.
What happens when a fallen angel is framed? Find
out in *A Midsummer Knight's Scream*.

Buy the whole series today!

Grab your next read here!
readerlinks.com/l/1893002

*Scan this QR Code with the camera on your phone.
You'll be taken right to the Magical Renaissance
Faire Mysteries series page. You can easily grab any
mysteries you've missed!*

GET YOUR FREE NOVELLA!

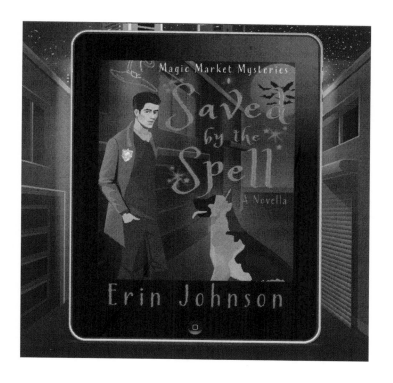

A magical academy. A suspicious death. Can an inexperienced cop expose the deadly secrets lurking behind bewitched classroom doors?

Download Saved by the Spell for FREE to solve a mystical murder today!
https://dl.bookfunnel.com/39ltzc764w

Thank You!

Trying out a new book is always a risk and we're thankful that you entered the Magical Renaissance Faire. If you loved this book, the most magical thing you can do (*even more magical than fairy dust*) is to leave a review so that other readers will take a chance on these Renaissance mysteries.

Don't feel you have to write a book report. A brief comment like, "Can't wait to read the next book in this series!" will help potential readers make their choice.

Leave a quick review HERE
https://readerlinks.com/l/1892987

Huzzah! We'll see you at the Faire!

Scan this QR Code with the camera on your phone. You'll be taken right to the review page for Much A'Broom About Nothing*!*

Other Books by Erin Johnson

The Magical Tea Room Mysteries

Minnie Wells is working her marketing magic to save the coziest, vampire-owned tea room in Bath, England. But add in a string of murders, spells to learn, and a handsome Mr. Darcy-esque boss, and Minnie's cup runneth over with mischief and mayhem.

Spelling the Tea
With Scream and Sugar
A Score to Kettle
English After-Doom Tea

The Spells & Caramels Paranormal Cozy Mysteries

Imogen Banks is struggling to make it as a baker and a new witch on the mysterious and magical island of Bijou Mer. With a princely beau, a snarky baking flame and a baker's dozen of hilarious, misfit friends, she'll need all the help she can get when the murder mysteries start piling up.

Seashells, Spells & Caramels
Black Arts, Tarts & Gypsy Carts
Mermaid Fins, Winds & Rolling Pins
Cookie Dough, Snow & Wands Aglow
Full Moons, Dunes & Macaroons

Airships, Crypts & Chocolate Chips
Due East, Beasts & Campfire Feasts
Grimoires, Spas & Chocolate Straws
Eclairs, Scares & Haunted Home Repairs
Bat Wings, Rings & Apron Strings
* Christmas Short Story: Snowflakes, Cakes &
Deadly Stakes

The Magic Market Paranormal Cozy Mysteries

A curse stole one witch's powers, but gave her the ability to speak with animals. Now Jolene helps a hunky police officer and his sassy, lie-detecting canine solve paranormal mysteries.

Pretty Little Fliers
Friday Night Bites
Game of Bones
Mouse of Cards
Pig Little Lies
Breaking Bat
The Squawking Dead
The Big Fang Theory

The Winter Witches of Holiday Haven

Running a funeral home in the world's most merry of cities has its downsides. For witch, Rudie Hollybrook, things can feel a little isolating. But when a murder rocks the festive town, Rudie's special skills might be the one thing that can help bring the killer to justice!

Cocoa Curses
Solstice Spirits

Special Collections
The Spells & Caramels Boxset Books 1-3
The Spells & Caramels Boxset Books 4-6
The Spells & Caramels Boxset Books 7-10
Pet Psychic Mysteries Boxset Books 1-4
Pet Psychic Mysteries Boxset Books 5-8

Want to hang out with Erin and other magical mystery readers?

Come join Erin's VIP reader group on Facebook: **Erin's Bewitching Bevy**. It's a cauldron of fun!

ABOUT THE AUTHOR

A native of Arizona, Erin loves her new home in the Pacific Northwest! She writes paranormal cozy mystery novels. These stories are mysterious, magical, and will hopefully make you laugh.

When not writing, she's hiking, napping with her dogs, and losing at trivia night.

You can find Erin at her website, **www.ErinJohnsonWrites.com** or on **Facebook**. Please email her at **erin@erinjohnsonwrites.com**. She loves to hear from readers!

Printed in Great Britain
by Amazon

66902574R00147